Brief Lives of Idiots

Brief Lives of Idiots

ERMANNO CAVAZZONI

TRANSLATED BY JAMIE RICHARDS

WAKEFIELD PRESS, CAMBRIDGE, MASSACHUSETTS

Wakefield Press, P.O. Box 425645, Cambridge, MA 02142

Originally published as *Vite brevi di idioti* in 1994.

This book was set in Garamond Premier Pro and Helvetica Neue Pro by Wakefield Press. Printed and bound by McNaughton & Gunn, Inc., in the United States of America.

ISBN: 978-1-939663-53-5

Available through D.A.P./Distributed Art Publishers
75 Broad Street, Suite 630
New York, New York 10004
Tel: (212) 627-1999
Fax: (212) 627-9484

10 9 8 7 6 5 4 3 2

CONTENTS

LONG LIVE THE IDIOTS

Originally published in Italian in 1994, *Brief Lives of Idiots* is an early book in Ermanno Cavazzoni's prolific career of genre-bending works between fiction, essay, and catalog. A smattering of his other titles gives a sense of his rather unusual interests: *Galaxy of the Demented*, *Hermits of the Desert*, *Useless Writers*, *Guide to Imaginary Animals*, *Natural History of Giants* (all of which await English translation).[1] An eccentric writer to be sure, Cavazzoni might be best considered alongside his fellow writers of the Po Valley: Gianni Celati, Daniele Benati, Ugo Cornia, Paolo Nori. Most of them are not well known, if at all, in English, but they share a minimalist style and a fascination with the incredible in the everyday. A member of the Oulipean-styled OpLePo, Cavazzoni is also an experimental writer who draws on literary constraints and formal play, like his Franco-American counterparts; and he is part of the Italian comic tradition, akin to such writers as Stefano Benni and Maurizio Salabelle. Overall, his work hearkens to other times, offering the kinds of curiosities one might encounter leafing through dusty incunabula or observing a seventeenth-century *Wunderkammer*, playing with the fantastic in the real and the real in the fantastic—and indeed, many of the tales here are drawn from or inspired by real-life stories found in institutional archives or forgotten old books and treatises.

The title *Brief Lives of Idiots* clearly evokes *The Lives of the Saints*, creating an implicit parallel between the two figures as examples of the marvelous and extraordinary, with the slight difference that idiots, unlike saints, cannot be delimited to the countable number implied by the definite article. The addition of "Brief" refers both to the length of the stories and the sense of "Life" as "animate existence," cut short for saintly and idiotic souls alike. Thus structured as a hagiography of the "simple," these stories are anecdotes or short biographies of one or more related idiots. Characters are generally described by name alone, some of which are real, and some of which are clever inventions. Cavazzoni takes inspiration and material for these tales from centuries-old medical tracts and mental asylum archives, and by picking out the fantastic, troubles the divisions between fact and fiction. It may seem unusual to liken idiots to saints, as Cavazzoni does explicitly in his "Note to the Reader." If a saint is defined as a person who is especially close to or similar to God, then the meaning of "saint" is dependent on one's concept of God or holiness. Many saints in the Christian canon were animated by an unflagging faith that they held no matter what, at the cost of great suffering and death. In regular people, such a trait would be decried as stubborn and stupid, and in fact most saints were only exalted postmortem. Similarly, Cavazzoni's idiots operate according to false, absurd, selfish, or pathological beliefs that often lead to their demise.

The book is also structured on traditional hagiography, which is typically organized by date (of birth or martyrdom) or in calendar form. Thus the thirty-one stories here make up a *menaion*, or month's worth, yet bear no specific dates that would limit or place the stories in time: valid for every calendar year, they may repeat ad infinitum. Each day depicts a different sort of idiot. And each week is punctuated by accounts of exceptional suicides on the seventh day, marking the day of (eternal) rest.

Partly in reference to the historical period when idiocy was officially classified as a mental illness, lunacy in both the sense of mutability and madness plays a certain role, and accordingly, the moon as its symbol looms large in Cavazzoni's imaginary. *The Nocturnal Library* takes place by moonlight; *The Voice of the Moon* recasts the idea of lunacy in the etymological sense of being in thrall to the moon (or "luna"); and of course, the "calendar month" structuring the *Brief Lives* corresponds to a single lunar cycle. In a 1997 interview, Cavazzoni traces a genealogy of lunar imagery in the Italian tradition, from Ariosto to Leopardi to Landolfi, and, of course, Fellini. He states that, for him, more than to the theme of folly or madness, the moon is related to idiocy, for the moon provides a point of view outside the world, observing all of it, measuring the finitude of all human action. And if death is all there is, our every act is quixotic, futile—idiotic. The moon can do nothing about it but stare blankly, like a head stuffed with straw.[2] The loss of sense is what creates the comic, absurd effect of our beautifully hopeless enterprises, the sound and fury of signifying nothing.

Cavazzoni's idiots run the gamut from the sublime to the banal to the obscene, suggesting multiple iterations and interpretations of the figure. The word "idiot" derives from the ancient Greek *ἰδιώτης* (*idiotes*, from the root word *idios*, or "one's own"), indicating a private citizen or common man, one who did not take part or have a role in political life, or perhaps a layperson without a professional trade. Put otherwise, it describes someone who keeps to themselves, who is of no use to the community. Whether and to what extent it was derogatory is a subject of debate for classicists, but for the contemporary reader this original use reveals a paradox buried within the word, and its difference from its apparent synonyms (stupid, moron, cretin, imbecile, ignoramus, etc.). One can be intelligent, competent, witty, and educated and still be an "idiotes" in the ancient sense—this accounts for the presence of engineers, scholars, and prodigies among Cavazzoni's idiots. One can even be political; an underlying theme running through several of the stories is a subtle critique of superficial adherence to ideology without true understanding—really the most common form of political participation in modern democratic societies.

Brief Lives of Idiots belongs to my own idiosyncratic canon of Italian writing, and I began translating it as part of a scouting project. The present book grew out of the publication of "The Albanians" and "Memories of Concentration Camp Survivors" in *World Literature Today* in 2011. At first the translating seemed straightforward enough. Detached narrative voice, paratactic style. As I went on, I came up against the complexity within this apparently simple style, as well as the particularity of Cavazzoni's highly readable yet slightly arcane language. Cavazzoni's brand of self-conscious simplicity is rare in contemporary Italian prose. Realism dominates, imposing a simplicity of another sort: "I saw Lila for the last time five years ago, in the winter of 2005." "I was just about to overtake Salvatore when I heard my sister scream." "Alice Della Rocca hated ski school."[3] These first lines of recent Italian bestsellers, in English translation, are virtually parodied by Cavazzoni's openers here: "Many claim that Jesus was an alien"; "An idiot by the name of Sereno Bastuzzi lived in a barn"; "What I'm about to tell you about Primo Apparuti is all true; he told it to me himself when he was in the asylum." Indeed, it is no coincidence that Cavazzoni includes "The Realist Writer" in his compendium of idiots; the critique of realism is nestled in every line. Cavazzoni's

English, then, needed to be simple, but alienatingly so. My motley stylistic analogues, from Michel Foucault to David Sedaris, really revolved around Samuel Beckett—perhaps not the most obvious model, but the writer most in the back of my mind as I went on to translate the rest of these idiot lives. For who is more sublimely idiotic than Vladimir or Estragon, or even the stone-sucking Molloy? A situational humor contained within minimalist language.

Just as Cavazzoni's work eschews realism, the idiot blithely stands in opposition to reality. Cavazzoni says: "The knights of Ariosto and the idiots I try to describe are like insects in a field. They have no sense of birth, life, death, transcendence, or God. . . . The idea of the beauty of living without seeing the sense of living has always appealed to me." At the periphery of these stories linger the grand categories of knowledge that are typically associated with modernity and human progress: science, technology, medicine. Yet the idiot doesn't know what to do with these things, or uses them imprecisely, improperly, exorbitantly, reverting to superstition, magic, nature. The persistence of the idiot disavows the dream of progress, and modernity in all its mythic grandeur is revealed to be a chimera. "I see [idiots] as only more evident examples of the universal behavior of all people," Cavazzoni has said. In case we thought we were immune, we are made to realize that idiocy is not an exception but the exemplum of the human condition par excellence. And so, these stories run the gamut of human experience. We have a variety of characters who, for one reason or another, are utterly unaware of their circumstances, but what unites them is the universality of their cluelessness.

Years in the making, little exercises in semiotics, this translation is dedicated to the sunbathers and the moongazers, and everyone in between.

Jamie Richards
Milan, 2020

NOTES

1. Other works of Cavazzoni's available in English include the 1991 bookish fantasy *Le tentazioni di Girolamo* (The Temptations of Jerome), published as *The Nocturnal Library* (tr. Alan Cameron, Vagabond Voices, 2010), and his most prominent work, *The Voice of the Moon* (translated by Ed Emery for Serpent's Tail in 1990, from *Il poema dei lunatici*, 1987), which formed the basis for Federico Fellini's final film.

2. See Peter Kuon and Hermann H. Wetzel, "Cavalieri, santi, lunatici, idioti . . . e scrittori inutili: A colloquio con Ermanno Cavazzoni," *Sonderdrück aus Italienisch* 38 (November 1997): 5–20.

3. These are the first lines from the following: Elena Ferrante, *Those Who Leave and Those Who Stay*, trans. Ann Goldstein (New York: Europa Editions, 2014); Niccolò Ammaniti, *I'm Not Scared*, trans. Jonathan Hunt (Edinburgh: Canongate, 2003); Paolo Giordano, *The Solitude of Prime Numbers*, trans. Shaun Whiteside (London: Transworld, 2009).

Brief Lives of Idiots

TO THE READER

What follows is one calendar month. Each day holds the life of a kind of saint, who experiences agony and ecstasy the way traditional saints do. Then our month ends, because everything in this world must end, even our brief idiot lives.

What month comes after, no one knows for sure; whether, for example, it will bring us laughter or tears, solitude or companionship. There is only conjecture. Some of it quite remarkable.

Some maintain that the month after never ends; this is a wild idea, it makes one tired just thinking about it.

Others say that we start over and over again, perhaps on another planet; yet each time humanity becomes a degree more idiotic. Until, in a slow progression, from planet to planet, complete and total idiocy is reached, and no one remembers a thing, not even the most basic, such as, for example, feeling any different from a rock or a meteorite. This, allegedly, is bliss.

It has been called a state very much like that of lead.

THE AERONAUTICAL EXPERT

Mr. Pigozzi once read in the newspaper about an East German, a mechanical engineer, who in 1976 built a small airplane with parts from old automobiles and fled to West Germany by flying over the border. Those were the days when the people were oppressed by communism.

Since Pigozzi had an old Fiat and didn't get along with his wife or his daughter, he started playing with the idea of taking off one day and never coming back. He was a mechanic and knew his way around an engine. He was also influenced by an illustrated geographical encyclopedia. His idea was to make the Fiat as light as possible, so he removed all the doors. He took off the rear wheels and added a small wheel he'd found at the scrap dealer's to the center. He made the driver's seat lighter and moved it to the middle, and got rid of the chassis and drive shaft. All that was left were the engine on the two front wheels, a pipe with the seat on it, and the wheel at the back. He took the car to the edge of town, where there was a big vacant field, waiting for a building permit to go through. Pigozzi kept it near the junkyard, but the worker there wasn't apprised of his plans; in fact, the junk dealer thought he was making a tractor for lawn mowing; at least that's what Pigozzi had told him—an experimental vehicle of futuristic conception. That's why it needed a propeller, and in fact, he had mounted one onto the drive shaft. He'd found the propeller at the airport, tossed in a corner; they gave it to him because it had a defect, but what that defect was escaped him. "At the airport," he told the junk dealer (Mr. Caravita), "you can find free propellers lying around; they have so many they just go to waste." Then he made wings out of canvas stretched over a light frame of metal rods. And a rudder over the wheel in the back. The junk dealer said that it looked like an airplane from the turn of the century; Pigozzi said it was actually a high-tech lawnmower like they have now in America.

Construction took over a year. He waited until the last day to attach the canvas so as not to draw attention; then suddenly, one morning around ten (in July 1978), he started the engine. All the gypsies in the gypsy camp noticed him do so; the engine had no muffler. He accelerated to full throttle and the airplane jerked into motion. It was pointed southwest.

It started to pick up speed. The junk dealer came out to look and it was already going very fast, by his account seventy or eighty kilometers per hour. The gypsies said a hundred. The field was on a slight incline and that facilitated the acceleration. It went faster and faster for nearly a kilometer. Most likely there was something wrong with the wings because it never lifted off. In any case, nobody saw exactly what happened. Besides, the junk dealer thought he was trying to mow the lawn. The gypsies ran after and found him dead, poor thing, against the side of the overpass. The plane was wrecked, but the Fiat engine and front Fiat tires were recognizable. The examination of Pigozzi afterward showed that he had been killed by the propeller. He had four million lire in his pocket, his driver's license, and a tube of condensed milk, perhaps for sustenance during the flight. He was also carrying a map of Asia.

According to the junk dealer's statement, his mistake was failing to include brakes: he hadn't considered the eventuality of stopping; but this would have been just as much of an issue with a lawnmower. His wife and daughter had known nothing of the matter, and the story they told everyone was that her husband (or father) died in an accident driving their Fiat 850 around a bend on the overpass. They thought he'd sold it ages ago; they didn't know he was still using it, even though it was old and unsafe. They put a small plaque at the bend, as people do for family members who die on the road. It had those lines engravers always use: "... by wife Virginia and daughter Sara, in loving memory ... et cetera, et cetera ... of Ettore Pigozzi."

THE THREE WISE MEN

Many claim that Jesus was an alien. Thus claimed Raffaello Pelagatti his entire life, i.e., from nineteen to about fifty, the age at which he died. This is an example of how one little idea thrown out there can ruin a person's life. He said that Jesus Christ was an alien who had probably fallen off a missile on Christmas night, or an illegal alien dumped by three hit men who had deboarded a spaceship dressed as the three wise men. The three wise men then reboarded; and indeed they were never heard from again.

With anything else, he was open to discussion and compromise, but not when it came to the three wise men. So, he said, in a certain sense Jesus had become bourgeois. Left at such a tender age, he had become just like other men; the three wise men, on the other hand, are more important for their racial purity. And someone should try to find out if they had ever come to dump anything else on Earth, and if so, whether they still touch down from time to time.

The problem was how to reconcile all this with Marxism, as Mr. Pelagatti was of the Marxist faith; he saw no inconsistencies in this. Nonetheless, he spent his entire life mired in controversy and incomprehension. When the Marxists said the wise men were a part of the superstructure, he found it to be extremely upsetting, and his immediate response was to lash out, especially at the theoreticians and more orthodox party members. He told the Marxists that ultimately he too was an atheist and that a spaceship didn't contradict Marxism, but actually extended it to outer space. Their biggest objection was usually the three camels. "Then why," said the cell secretary, known as Siccardi, "why do the three wise men come on camels and not rockets?" Pelagatti's response was that Marxism had unsubstantiated preconceived notions about camels, and what did they know about extraterrestrial propulsion systems anyway? Those were years of intense political stringency where they strictly followed Engels and Marx, so people easily came to blows over who was in the right and who in the wrong. In 1952, Pelagatti got a broken arm, his left; a few months later he broke the arm of a priest. What happened was that whatever the Marxists did to him in a meeting, he would turn around and do to the priests. It was a form of psychological compensation, another product of the era, as if priests existed for Marxists to vent their neuroses on. He even lost a few teeth defending his theory of the three wise men; but more often than not, after a brief exchange of ideas, the group leaders and the secretary himself threw him to the ground and held him as he thrashed about, punching and swiping pell-mell. But it was one against a mob, so ultimately the latter won out, shutting him up so they could go on with their political meeting. So the day afterward an angry Pelagatti would go looking for priests, though he only needed one to settle the score. "The three wise men traveled on rockets," he'd say. This usually frightened the priest, and upon hearing it he would try to flee as fast as he could, for Pelagatti was notorious for being the sworn enemy of the priesthood. Pelagatti demanded a theological debate, but it was finished before it could begin, for the priest's face immediately revealed his conservative and conformist ideas about the three wise men. The priest would sometimes barricade himself in the confessional and Pelagatti would heckle him from outside: "Who are the three wise men?" he'd say, and you could hear his fists pounding on the wood to drive the priest out of his hiding spot. It should be said that if the priest was alone, Pelagatti was able to overtake him, since confessionals are made of light wood; but a clergyman was rarely to be found alone, and indeed his backup, clerics or congregants, would rush over and Pelagatti would back off. "I just want to know," he'd say, "why you reject even the possibility of spaceships." They knew that Pelagatti was a Marxist and this set him apart. Thus Pelagatti remained a loner throughout his life; he was frequently taken down to the police station, and subject to political identity crises that would plunge him either into obstinate silence or vaniloquence about the rocket engines and camels of the three wise men.

Around 1960 a curious thing happened; in one of his sorties against the priests, Pelagatti came across one who was, in a manner of speaking, his final cure. And it's even more curious that this priest, as if in some kind of cosmic joke, was called Don Pelacani—showing that skinning a dog isn't so different from skinning a cat. Don Pelacani used to be a pastor at a church outside of town, but was now retired from holy service and advanced in age; he was a big smoker and he had a theory. He said that Engels and Marx had been made up by the Marxists and according to him had never existed; you could tell by their photographs, because their beards were fake, probably rented. He supposed a couple of random, anonymous Marxists had invented them, probably two brothers after a day of partying with all the other Marxists. They had, he said, put on beards and introduced themselves to the photographer as Engels and Marx. And as it benefited the entire Marxist movement, their portraits had been paraded around ever since, even though the beards were obviously fake, glued on or tied on with string, and it was obvious that brothers or twins were behind the pseudonyms Engels and Marx.

Don Pelacani and Mr. Pelagatti would go on walks, and they would be calm. They would discuss the three wise men or Engels and Marx, but each without interfering in the theory of the other; they had an unspoken pact to democratically respect each other's field of expertise. You would often see them sitting silently on a bench. It's funny that one was called Pelagatti and the other Pelacani, but they lived in Varese until at least 1965.

THE SCALABRINI FAMILY

Renato Scalabrini has always had this habit, for example, of throwing a stone in the air and standing there watching it fall. If the stone hits his head he whimpers. "Look how stupid you are," the neighbors say. But after a while he'll do it all over again, as if he wants to better understand the phenomenon. He'll throw the stones so high sometimes he loses sight of them, and then they'll suddenly land on his head. Those are the ones that hurt the most. He'll study the particular stone to see if it's the same one he tossed up. "Renato, come here," someone'll say to get him to stop. And that's often enough to distract him from the stones, because he's a meek and mild-tempered man.

He is the eldest of five brothers; now he is fifty-two years old, but he's always had this habit. He's a member of the Scalabrini family, but they're not all stupid: there's an uncle who's slightly less so. In fact, he drives a car and often takes his nephews along. The boys love the car, and when they're in the car they're all quiet watching their uncle drive. The uncle likes to go slow, but the car tends to get away from him, especially on straight roads, where the tires somehow find their way into the ditch all by themselves. Once the car even flipped over. Actually, more than once. The uncle says it's because it picks up so much speed going downhill. It's very exciting for his nephews, who later tell the story as a special and wonderful experience.

They often take little trips like this. They'll go to the river for a swim, for instance. When Renato sees the riverbed covered in stones, he squeals in delight. But it's not the water he's excited about. His brothers, unlike him, race into the water, some so happy they go under. Especially one, Sebastiano, the youngest; he's forty, but acts like he's ten. He likes shouting and jumping in the water so much that after a while, in his glee, he flips over, and flailing about he inhales water, but as if he's just playing. The uncle fishes him out and gets him to throw up. But seeing his brothers still in the water bouncing around and throwing mud at each other, he can't lie still on the shore and before he's fully recovered he gets excited again and starts laughing. The brothers pull him back in and jump all over him because he's short, until the uncle has to intervene and make him throw up again. This uncle is a fisherman, and when they've all had enough of the water, he goes to fish.

Meanwhile, Renato amuses himself playing with the stones. He takes one and tosses it in the air. He throws it straight up and stands there watching. As usual it falls on his head, or his face. Or it falls on his brothers, who whimper and rub their heads. After their swim the brothers lie out, their bellies bloated. One of them, the second oldest, Dario, aged fifty, usually lies on Sebastiano. Or he'll lie on Toni, the second youngest. These are family habits. He does it to be more comfortable, even though the others don't like it and complain. So if a stone falls on them they panic, looking up and all around. They see Renato in the distance and don't make the connection. To them, it's a mystery of the river. Every now and then the stone will fall on the uncle while he's fishing and spook the fish. So he'll motion to Renato to keep quiet and move further away. He also gestures that if he doesn't, he's going to be in big trouble. Once Renato even found an old flat iron and tossed it up in the air; it fell on the uncle, who was hurt and had to stop fishing.

Renato has had this particular tendency since childhood. As a boy, playing meant throwing toys in the air. When they fell on the ground he would sit and study them for a long time, especially if they had been damaged. He studied them when they fell on his head too, but with the air of someone suffering injustice on account of knowledge. It's a family of loons, some said; it's a family of morons, said others, especially those who'd taken stones to the head.

4

THE PYROMANIACS

The following is not a case of a typical firestarter.

The typical firestarter, or pyromaniac, feels a rush throughout their entire body at the thought or sight of fire, and often takes orders from fire as if they were a servant to it. Pyromaniacs are generally small in stature and beady-eyed, and worship fire as a god. Bruno Primavera, however, was very tall, far above average, and had a long, tapered head without much of a cranium. Yet this bore no repercussions on his mental capacity or verbal expressivity, which was clear, if a bit slow and halting. When he inherited his parents' house, he locked himself inside for three days; on the third day the house burned down, and thus he lost his entire inheritance. Rueful, he went around with ash in his pockets; for this, he was considered unhinged, but he did it in memory of his parents and all that he had left of them. He had locked himself in the house to take inventory and in his mourning hadn't wanted company. The house was in great disarray and birds had made nests in the windows and fireplace. He later stated that there was some loose straw in the barn mixed with eggshells that had started to rot. He made it into a pile to tidy up, and since he had some matches in his pocket he instinctively went to light it on fire, as you do with leftovers from the field. But the moment he did so, the barn caught fire with such a violent burst that the house burned down too. He wasn't able to call for help in time. The house, he said, was very dry and probably flammable.

One day, he was sitting in front of the stove; this was two months later, and he was at his sister's, stoking the fire with the tongs. Then he started to pick up individual embers and would spend some time sitting and looking at them. For example, he'd blow on one and then observe the effect. At some point a piece of charcoal fell under the rug; instead of grabbing it with the tongs and throwing it back into the fire, he saw a bottle of alcohol on the table and stupidly poured it on to extinguish it; thus the rug caught fire. He knew that alcohol was highly flammable, but in the moment it didn't occur to him. "I was distracted," he said. "I mistook it for water." Then, in shock, he dropped the bottle, and the fire spread to the wood floor. To avoid another blunder, he ran out of the room; the fire shattered the windows and the whole building came down. He called it bad luck, though luckily nobody had died; some children had just suffered smoke inhalation.

After that, he lived in a small flat of his own; and as he was boiling water to make soup, he observed the gas flame. With a scrap of paper, he lit a second burner, then a third, then all four, because he enjoyed the sight: it was rare for all four burners to be going at the same time. But in the meantime the scrap of paper found its way to a newspaper, then the newspaper to a curtain; there were some straw baskets and they too caught fire, and also the tablecloth, probably made out of flammable polyurethane; until the whole kitchen, the brooms, the towels, the pinewood credenza, was on fire. By some miracle the house didn't burn, because the neighbors rushed over with buckets and saved him, although they couldn't save the rooms he owned. He, Primavera, was singed from head to toe, and imbued with smoke, but had no burns that would require a trip to the hospital. Without hair, it looked as though he had not so much a head as a plateau.

His only problem, one could say, was that he was very fond of matches; he liked to light them and watch them burn until the flame brushed his fingers. On occasion he would get burned, or almost so, and have to toss them away; usually nothing happened, unless he happened to be around leaves or trees, or near sulfur, or tinder, or the fuel reservoir for the tractors; or places soaked in gas due to a leak. But that's not pyromania, because a pyromaniac craves fire or seeks it out, by any means necessary; for pyromaniacs, fire is never accidental or the result of carelessness or mild stupidity.

His sister, Adelaide Soliani (née Primavera), remembered her brother always having displayed this vice of lighting matches and staring at them. He'd carried matches on him from a very young age; in fact, once he scraped them with his fingernail until they ignited right in his pocket, burning his pants and getting him expelled, as this was during class, where he had already inadvertently set a few small fires in his binder or someone else's. His notebooks always had blackened edges and he'd melted his Bakelite pen for fun. He liked to light matches in the dark. He would light as many as three or four at a time, even under the covers, where he would make a tent and what he called a boy-scout campfire. He'd had no fire safety instruction at home, as neither his mother nor his father had ever worried about matches. Even though fires were constantly breaking out.

An experimental psychologist, Dr. Magnacucchi, having learned of the case and suspecting a serious form of pyromania, wanted to conduct a special study on Primavera. So he held daily sessions with him at his office, as Primavera had a court order to seek treatment. He observed him through a two-way mirror and took notes, because his method consisted of observing patients through two-way mirrors while they were in the waiting room. He wanted to catch the moment when Primavera was struck by an overwhelming urge to light a match and set the room on fire. He had a fire extinguisher ready in case. But Primavera waffled. Sitting in a chair, he would light a match, and melancholically watch it burn. At most he would light two at once. The rest of the time, when he wasn't lighting matches, he was perfectly well-mannered; occasionally, he scratched his head. A strange thing he did do was go up to the mirror, just centimeters away from Dr. Magnacucchi with his chair and table, look at his face, and finding any longish hairs in his beard, burn them with a match. It was interesting, but not quite enough for Dr. Magnacucchi to write a research thesis of scientific value on "unconscious volatility in pyromaniacs"—he had already decided on the title. He waited for the urge to be unleashed, or to see Primavera in a trance, a slave to fire, in the grip of voices. Instead, after burning his hair he just sat back down and started picking his teeth with his nail, lost in thought, or so it seemed. The doctor even left some rubbing alcohol on the table to move things along, and left him alone for hours, since anyone with matches would have done something with them out of boredom: little rockets, smoke, jet jets. Whereas Primavera was engrossed merely by a match in his mouth, and Dr. Magnacucchi on the other side of the mirror sat waiting. Then when he brought him in to talk, Primavera denied being a pyromaniac; he said that he'd had a lot of accidents, and that he kept matches in his pocket for contingencies, like if the gas needed igniting, and every now and then he'd strike one up for fun. "I burn a few to test them," he said, "if ever the need to light a wood stove or gas burner should suddenly arise." Therefore, the study did not progress. It would have been impossible to put this banal nonsense into a specialist thesis, or write about a pyromaniac scratching his head. Then a fire broke out. Dr. Magnacucchi smoked a pipe; watching Primavera sit there doing nothing, one day after lunch he nodded off over his notes and his pipe set them on fire. He woke up in a blaze because it was parchment paper. For a moment the situation was very dangerous, because flaming papers were flying about everywhere. On the other side of the mirror Primavera had paused to listen. Fortunately there was nothing too flammable; the alcohol was on the table in the other room. Once he'd composed himself, he snuffed out the last sparks with the fire extinguisher; he'd also burned one of his sleeves and his beard. Dr. Magnacucchi told the magistrate that it was a risky case to study, because Primavera was a surreptitious pyromaniac and not a typical pyromaniac. Hence he eluded scientific observation.

LUIGI PIERINI, CALCULATING PRODIGY

Calculating prodigies are people who calculate prodigiously fast. Occasionally they find themselves in asylums, psychiatric hospitals, when the calculations won't stop and their head is so consumed by numbers that they forget to sleep, eat, or talk to other people. Sometimes they perform on stage, like the famous Giacomo Inaudi in the late 1800s, or Ugo Zaneboni, a police officer, not as fast as Inaudi, but able to answer any number-related question before an audience. He also knew the train table by heart and could recite a list of two hundred and fifty numbers forward and backward. He debuted in Milan at the Eden Theater, and for years toured Italy with moderate success; he was considered second to Inaudi.

Luigi Pierini could also be considered a calculating prodigy, but he didn't become famous. He was born in Pomarance on 12 December 1878 to an uneducated family; he'd been slightly lame since childhood and was a stable boy. He grew up completely illiterate. When he was eleven another stable boy taught him to count to a hundred. He was so taken with it that he started counting constantly, mostly out loud but silently as well. Within a short time he made it to ten thousand, with virtually no help, and then much further. In the idleness of pastoral life he counted everything and this was his favorite activity. A priest taught him the four basic operations and after mass he would stop with the farmers outside the church and calculate how many seconds of life each had lived or how many hours had passed since the birth of Christ; upon request, he'd do any multiplication or division problem up to eight integers. As he returned to his sheep, he would count his steps, and he liberally practiced the different operations, in a mental effort that was constant yet very satisfying.

He was discovered by Mr. Lessi, a schoolteacher in Pomarance. One evening at the cafe, Luigi Pierini correctly divided 150 billion by 1,654 in front of everyone. So Mr. Lessi told him: "Which number mutliplied by itself would equal 180,625?" Luigi Pierini thought for a moment and said: "425." Thus he learned square roots and all night long he pulled out some really tough ones. The teacher Lessi wrote in the Volterra *Corazziere* dated 4 July 1892 that in Pomarance there was a calculating phenomenon, almost equal to the famous Inaudi.

Some time later, Luigi Pierini went to Grosseto, where Inaudi had performed at a theater, certain he could do the same. He referenced Mr. Lessi's comments as qualification. But he was turned away. He moved on to Massa Marittima, to Viterbo, then to Rome. He had the clipping from the *Corazziere*, which as an illiterate he couldn't read, but he recited parts from memory; he would always mention Mr. Lessi and at first opportunity pull out a few square roots. On these trips his greatest suffering was hunger; he went up to thirty hours without eating. Then he found someone who, upon hearing his calculations and letting him do them at a café for the customers, was amazed and offered him a bowl of minestra. He joined up with a pair of vagabonds who exhibited him in smaller towns as an extraordinary phenomenon; with them he managed to earn a few lire.

Then he was examined by Professor Mantegazza who studied calculating prodigies and had also studied Inaudi and Zaneboni. He found that having been left on his own, he had not been able to perfect his skills, but he did say that he incontestably had calculating talent. He had him perform a great number of calculations at his laboratory in Florence, recording how much time he took and comparing his results to Inaudi's. Then he measured his face and found an asymmetry and a sizeable cranial deformation. Outside of numbers, he seemed very mentally confused; he spoke of himself vaguely, with a very limited vocabulary; he didn't remember the names of the cities he had been to, and he couldn't say a word about Rome. Every four or five words, in order to sound important, he liked to repeat, "essentially." He mentioned the sea, astronomy, and said he loved poetry: he claimed to have written a beautiful poem himself.

After his experience with Mantegazza, he became much more conceited; he spoke of Inaudi as if they knew each other and together with Mantegazza constituted a trio of dear friends. He said that they were the official geniuses of mathematics. So he took care to dress nicely; he went around the countryside absorbed in calculations, but also in his poem, which he constantly pruned and polished, making him even more vain. He appeared in Tuscan cafes where he tried to give performances doing calculations, but especially where he recited his long-touted poem, which went like this:

Fair Florentia, mother of sciences
for which thou wast the brightest star;
shining light on the ten alliances
of ingenuity, tale-telling, and art.
Indeed, so noble, gentle, and courtly thee,
that to paradise thou havest still the key.

When Mantegazza heard this in his laboratory, he quickly classified Luigi Pierini as a simple idiot.

THE ENEMY OF SPEED

Once there was a man who couldn't get over the speed at which the Earth travels. "Do you know how fast we're going?" he would say whenever anyone noticed his worried look. "108,000 kilometers an hour, do you realize?" Because of this, he said, he wasn't comfortable going on working while the Earth shot through space at such an insane speed with us here like a bunch of numbskulls at its mercy. He said that everyone, his coworkers first and foremost, acted irresponsibly. They'd go out dancing, or get married like it's nothing, all happy, as the Earth careens unchecked through space, and no one knows where it could wind up at any moment. "We're a bunch of nuts," he said. "In theory we should be wearing safety belts; instead we go to the office and they give us chairs that break just from being looked at. The chairs don't really matter," he said. "They're just an example of how shamefully irresponsible these companies are, as are the rest of us, even the unions." Then he said that if the Earth rose in the stratosphere even a few kilometers, the temperature would drop to negative 55 degrees centigrade; therefore, it's a miracle, at the speed we're going, that we don't suddenly get blasted by a glacial wind that fireplaces and radiators would be no match for. "I'd like to see," he said, "all those people who spend all summer at the beach! All those dingbats in accounting, like Ms. Cammelli, who sunbathe in the nude; let's see how fun that is at 55 degrees below zero! And at 108,000 kilometers an hour!" He said he couldn't just sit in his office pretending like nothing was going on like those fools, and he often took sick days on which he would feverishly study a star map, worrying and agonizing over the ever imminent possibility of colliding with wayward asteroids, they too flying like fireballs in all directions, or running into the space dust he'd always heard so much about, which would be terrifying at this speed, or a toxic comet tail made up of cyanide with its characteristic bitter almond smell.

He said that anyway if there was a God he was a kook, and a cynic, who put people's lives—i.e., ours—in danger, making us race along at 108,000 kilometers an hour, essentially in total darkness, amid the convulsive traffic of other celestial bodies hurling through space unregulated without the possibility of aborting at the last second, just advancing blindly toward destruction.

He could no longer sleep at night because he was clinging to the mattress, listening for the explosion. So said his wife, who unlike him was able to sleep, but was disturbed by her husband's constant flinching whenever he happened to hear the building door slam, or a creak, or a chair scrape the floor overhead. His wife tossed and turned, and he would say "stop making noise," because he was afraid of not hearing in time, say, the Earth colliding with another planet orbiting in the opposite direction. He was afraid of getting suddenly flung from the bed, even though he realized it was irrational, because if that happened the house would cave in too, at the very least; maybe even the city would be razed to the ground. During the day he always kept his eyes half-shut and his head down, like someone riding a motorcycle with the wind in his face. He even sat in his office chair like a biker, and always wore a neck scarf in summer and winter, tied very tightly so as not to catch a draft. In fact, he suffered from colds and sciatica, and he always cursed the blasts of air that hit him. Other times he felt like the ceiling was about to come crashing down on him and he feared for his neck and spine; thus he was tense and bundled up, and if he had to write, he wrote quickly in fear of not making it to the end of the sentence. This was his very agitated and tormented office life at the Paltrinieri & Becchi metal shelving company.

"We're riding a cannonball," he said, "with one, very simple prospect; it's a matter of time, even hours or minutes." And his wife, who was tired of this obsession, would sometimes try to calm him down, saying: "Want to bet we don't crash into anything?" He would reply that it was an idiotic thing to say, completely blithe, like betting on someone speeding down Corso Vittorio Emanuele at 900 kilometers per hour, i.e., jet speed:

"Want to bet nothing happens to him?" His wife got annoyed, he got scared by his own words and broke into a sweat, and he put on a wood helmet that made him look like a miner even though he knew it was useless, as it was an antique and for cycling; but it helped him devote himself more intently to studying the star map. He was especially afraid of certain small, rarely mentioned planets with elliptical orbits that intersect with ours, about which he informed himself weekly by telephone calls with the astrophysics department at the university. Most of all he was troubled by a certain Adonis; he would ask where it was at that moment, if it was visible by telescope, and from the tone of their reply he could tell whether they were lying or telling him the truth, because they would say, for example, that their ephemerides weren't really up to date, or that Adonis didn't reach magnitude eleven in that period; or that they couldn't readily give data over the phone to just anybody, and that was the response that alarmed him the most, but it was also the most frequent. So he'd go for a walk on the streets around the astrophysics building, sometimes going inside on some pretense and scanning the custodians' faces to figure out if the alarm had gone off, if there was a leak, if, say, an interplanetary catastrophe was imminent. He also waited for the professors to come out to see how they acted—if they were nervous, conferring nervously, or fleeing en masse. Once he saw a disheveled professor with a suitcase leave a classroom, hop in his car, and speed off. He got really scared and started asking, "What's going on? Tell me what's going on!" And he grabbed an assistant by the lapels, crying and begging. Or he'd follow professors on the street, especially when they were in pairs, to catch bits of their conversation, maybe even something about Adonis's trajectory. But apparently he never caught anything except for regular chitchat, so he decided they were speaking in code. He expected to arrive at the university one day to find it deserted, everyone hiding out in atomic shelters unbeknownst to the human race, because an unidentified asteroid from a runaway galaxy was moving at the speed of light—no, that was impossible, he said to himself, because of the theory of relativity; anyway, it was heading at an incommensurable speed toward Earth, and Earth was going toward it at 108,000 kilometers an hour. Not to mention the fact that the entire solar system (and us like idiots along with it, bound to the same suicidal fate) was traveling at 72,000 kilometers an hour toward the Vega star in the constellation Lyra. No one knows what's in between, perhaps opaque matter that'll drop on us like a bomb of rock or cement. What fun that'll be, with the skyscrapers, the suspension bridges, the highway viaducts built solely out of human stupidity; what fun with the windows, even the shatterproof ones at the Paltrinieri & Becchi metal shelving company. But he got scared just seeing an astrophysicist standing at the window to check if it was raining. He revered astrophysicists.

His son, his only child, had left home at eighteen because he'd never gotten along with his father. He thought his father was deranged and they'd had plenty of heated discussions about speed in general, because he liked going fast on motorcycles, whereas his father said that motorcycles were extremely dangerous, moving in a precarious and unnatural balance, and everyone who rides a motorcycle is destined to fall; therefore, he wouldn't take the responsibility of buying him one, because it would have added to the danger that we already constantly face in hurtling through space at 108,000 kilometers an hour. "You should be happy," he yelled at his son, "if you're in such a hurry, if you like going fast!" Then the son bought a motorcycle for himself and almost immediately skidded off the road at a curve; the father went to the hospital to see him, and only said he hadn't known the force of inertia on a body in motion. The son bought himself another motorcycle, but he didn't know how to drive like a regular person, he just wanted to go fast, it was built into his psyche, and luckily for him, he ran into a chain-link fence that saved him.

The son's escapades distracted the father somewhat, also because his wife would worry all day, and when they heard an ambulance go by she'd say that something had happened, she could feel it, and she wanted her husband to call all the hospitals or check the emergency room to relieve her anxiety. Thus the speed of the Earth shifted to lower priority, or at least was something he now kept to himself. And looking over the map, he was comforted, for example, by Jupiter's distance and the fact that it was gassy, like an air bubble or cloud. Pluto, Neptune, Uranus, and Saturn comforted him too. Distance in general comforted him; as did galaxies, and the fact that, fortunately, the universe was still expanding. But he couldn't understand the reason for such speed, for what benefit; why so much toil and haste in the skies. Even the moon calmed him somewhat; but he didn't understand it, and he saw it the way a philosopher would, as an inanimate object traveling at breakneck speed, and couldn't be convinced otherwise; and he gave it the same harsh judgment he did his son.

These fears came back to him from time to time in August, especially on San Lorenzo, the night of the shooting stars. It was like being, he said, a deaf person in a bombing, and what's more, he said, you didn't even know what war it was.

This family's surname was Vacondio, and they lived on Via Po in Turin.

WORKING SUICIDES

On 3 January 1980, at five p.m., a tailor from Anagni, tired of working as a tailor, locked himself in the back room of his shop and hanged himself with measuring tape.

In mid-February, a housepainter drank a jar of paint thinner and died at the hospital after a day of agony. He had convinced himself that while he was out painting his wife was regularly receiving male callers at home.

One March, a traffic officer suddenly jumped off his platform in front of a passing ambulance with its sirens blaring and died on impact. He had been complaining about his job for years. He complained about the noise of the cars and the smog.

A professor of Roman law provoked a nervous student so much during an exam that the latter grabbed the gavel on his desk and hit him in the face and then the temple. The professor had wanted to die for some time; he said no one needed Roman law anymore and that it only served to torture professors and students from generation to generation.

An auto mechanic locked himself in a car on 5 April and starved to death. He wasn't married because he'd lost a hand fixing an engine; this, he said, was a shortcoming that women noticed right off the bat.

A saleswoman at a fur shop locked herself in a closet full of mothballs one Saturday night. Since the shop was closed through Monday, she died from inhaling the fumes. A note cursing the shop owner was found beside her.

A television director, during the shooting of a low-budget show with very few actors, was found dead in a cast-iron chair that appeared in every scene that had been made into a high-voltage electric chair. Apparently production was required to skimp on everything, even lighting.

One night a suburban priest who suffered from atherosclerosis lit several candles and took several capsules of frankincense, which is a strong vasoconstrictor, perhaps thinking it was a vasodilator. Therefore, at approximately four a.m. he had an ischemic stroke and died. However, the fact that he owned a pharmaceutical reference book suggests that he was aware of the effect of frankincense on coronary arteries.

During a party rally in July, a male politician from the province of Bergamo fell off the stage and died. The stage was much higher than a normal stage, and very narrow. An investigation was opened to establish whether he had been pushed or had jumped to commit suicide.

During the dog days of August, a bicycle mechanic hanged himself with a tire; apparently, motivated by the heat.

One night an asthmatic union official returned to the union offices where he died of asphyxiation. He had been retired for years and was found face down on the conference table in the morning. He had developed asthma going to union meetings because of the constant pipe and cigarette smoke, to which he was allergic.

A professional photographer poisoned himself with silver nitrate as a result of an overexposed photograph that didn't live up to his idea of art. Silver nitrate was used by the pioneers of photography, and it poisons the blood.

A beekeeper knew that a bee sting can trigger anaphylactic shock, and he always said to his wife: "I'm going to kill myself," because he wasn't satisfied at home or with his trade. When he died on 8 September from a bee sting, his wife, when asked, called it a suicide. But the investigating judge dismissed the case because it was unsolvable.

A poet who composed meaningless poems using a calculator committed suicide by gas inhalation to give his poetry a general sense of drama. But the police report simply states that he left the gas on, possibly by accident.

A plumber having a major nervous breakdown jumped into a canal with pipes tied around his neck with a total weight of twenty-two kilos.

One afternoon, a sixty-three-year-old animal trainer, tired of circus life, went into the tiger cage dressed as a monkey. The tigers weren't ferocious, but not recognizing him, mauled him to death. The case was registered as a suicide.

A young but ailing gravedigger had himself buried in a dead man's place, slipping into the coffin before it was sealed. The dead man was found a week later at his house under the bed.

THE PRESSURE TAKER

A tenant farmer who lived with his mother, in a house near the country road, in a valley between the mountains, spent his days hiding in the bushes because he imagined that's what doctors do. He would pop out when he saw someone pass by and offer to take their blood pressure for free. His name was Sauro Gallinari, but everyone called him Gallinari. He kept a blood pressure gauge beside him in the fields, and as he tended to his rented field of oats or potatoes he thought of nothing but medicine, for which he believed he had natural talent. Whereas the land, he said, was his serfdom and was of no import to the course of his life. He tried it out on himself during the siesta hour, as he had heard hospital doctors do when an instrument isn't yet perfected, and would take his time measuring his blood pressure, sitting in the shade of a tree, greatly satisfied. He pumped the blood pressure gauge as hard as he could, until his arm fell asleep; he tried to resist, because in his opinion a blood pressure test was a kind of test of strength that was good for one's long-term health. Gallinari was very heavyset, with an unusual wrinkle on his forehead that made him look serious, like a country doctor from the 1800s. But he had a very short neck and his head was squashed between his shoulders like that of a gorilla.

He had found a doctor's bag in the cellar when he came to live in Sologno in 1952; inside there was some equipment from before the war, and he was so pleased he thought he'd struck gold and would quickly be able to go into practice, specializing in blood pressure measurement, the branch of medicine he preferred and that came to him most easily. The thermometer didn't appeal to him as a specialty, because it didn't inflate or have a variety of applications apt for each individual case; in other words, it was ultimately fragile and not very versatile, in his estimation. Nonetheless he looked for farmers alone in the fields and measured their temperature in order to gain experience and also to promote himself. If someone agreed, then he would take advantage and look inside their mouth for free, and then try to stick a spoon down their throat to make them gag. But if there were several farmers together, they usually mocked him, deriding the thermometer and blood pressure gauge he always carried; for example, they tried to take them for fun, saying they were fake contraptions, tricks he'd made up that didn't cure anything. They even threw clods of dirt at him to make each other laugh, and once a rock at his head, out of pure collective ignorance and stupidity. This was why Gallinari avoided groups of people and bars and preferred individuals, who were generally more open to medicine. He went around his house with a stethoscope hanging off his ears, despotically ordering his mother around, like doctors do with their patients. He forced his mother to stay in bed like a chronic invalid under observation. She actually was an old lady, a little weak in both body and mind, and she'd just make herself some soup and return to her room as if she lived in a retirement home. Gallinari took her pressure every day with an air of great importance. He would wrap the cuff around her arm, her leg, or wherever inspiration suggested, and inflate it, continuing to inflate it even after his mother complained. His mother thought it was treatment, and so she was patient and submissive; moreover, it wasn't clear to her that he was her son; she thought she recognized him at certain moments, but as he inflated the blood pressure cuff with a white smock around his waist and gauze over his mouth, she looked at him and had flashbacks of a dentist from her childhood.

In addition, Gallinari gave injections with a makeshift wooden stick; he did them for a woman who crossed his fields to reach the street: Signora Zagno, who volunteered herself for fun and not medical advancement as he claimed in some confused statements. He'd have her lie down in a ditch, expose her buttocks, then give her a shot with a blade of grass or a dry twig. Sometimes he would hit her knees with a hammer, his scythe hammer, while having her say "aaaah." She laughed, unlike him, as he was on the job. Then he went back to working in the fields and dismissed Signora Zagno with a certain self-importance.

He also practiced on a neighbor, a sharecropper named Salvioli; he treated him with the thermometer in the cornfield. He had him hold it in his mouth every day, a little longer each time; then he ran his stethoscope over his neck and back. This Salvioli, who had arthritis, said that he could feel the benefits all through his torso. Not a complete cure, but some benefits; also with his breathing, as he was a longtime sufferer of asthma. And this was a sort of personal victory against the backwardness of peasants, who all had arthritis and didn't want to get treated. So after a while they no longer threw rocks or dirt at him, but wanted a little of the progress and wellness Salvioli kept talking about; therefore, during this time Gallinari could consider himself the valley's general practitioner.

Yet his career was cut short due to a stroke of bad luck. One evening, he had placed, according to his treatment system, his blood pressure gauge around his mother's neck and inflated it so much that his mother suffocated: she was already quite old and her whimpering had likely been inaudible. This happened in 1956, when Gallinari was forty-two and his mother seventy-five. Gallinari said that it wasn't bad luck and that he had actually extended her life by taking her blood pressure. All this, however, was not so clear in court, or at least Gallinari didn't make it clear enough; therefore his medical bag was confiscated and put into evidence. It was deemed an erroneous application of first aid, for which he was acquitted of the charge of premeditated voluntary manslaughter; yet he was barred from the practice of medicine and all related activity, as he had no degree and wasn't licensed by the medical board. He went back to working his land in Sologno. All he had left was a tourniquet that he secretly used in the fields on various parts of Signora Zagno's body, also continuing to give her shots with whatever materials he happened upon in the fields, like pine needles, sticks, blades of hay or straw. These sessions were always conducted in secret and went on for a number of years.

9

THE ALBANIANS

Naldo Govi worked at the city pound. One afternoon, a dog escaped from the pound; they ran after him, uphill, for an hour and a half, he and one of the dogcatchers; they caught up to him at the top of a hill, but the dog resisted and bit Govi on the shin. This probably knocked him off balance, or maybe he'd already been unbalanced for a while. He went home and said to his wife: "Hello? Can I help you?" His wife replied: "The village idiot is back already?" She often used this expression in their conversations. He looked at her. She didn't look familiar; his wife was no beauty. So Govi thought: "This woman is crazy, I'd better humor her." Indeed, his wife's hair was unkempt and she was wearing the old housecoat she'd put on to clean. Basically, she didn't look very proper. "This is some crazy vagrant," he thought, "who thinks she lives here." Govi said nothing more because he'd started to feel a burning sensation in his stomach. In the kitchen there was a young man—it was his son, but he didn't recognize him. He assumed he'd wandered in with the woman. This young man, however, didn't even turn to greet him; he was eating something, some cheese.

Govi didn't kick them out because he thought maybe there was some other fact he wasn't remembering. For example, how they happened to have keys to the house. And why they weren't afraid of him. In fact, they acted like it was their house.

So from that day on, every morning he woke up to find those people in the kitchen; he was especially disgusted by the young man, with his peach fuzz and pimply face. But he just acted normal. The woman always seemed to worry that the young man didn't eat enough. These people were his family, but he didn't know them anymore. Sometimes he would say something about the coffee, meanwhile observing them as they spread butter on their toast and the boy ate some sausage.

For a while he thought they were from Albania, and that he had somehow signed an agreement to host them. He had actually signed something in support of refugees, he remembered that, and his coworker at the pound, Zamboni, remembered it too. Govi told him: "There are refugees in my house, a man and a woman." Zamboni said: "Well, you signed up for it."

His family didn't realize that he no longer knew who they were; his talk just seemed a little more vague. His wife had always thought he was a pathetic idiot, and she'd always told him as much; lately, he just seemed even more so.

Then, due to his peptic ulcer, Govi called for the doctor, Dr. Prini—the one who referred this case, which would have otherwise remained unknown (and unimaginable). "Those people are in there," he told the doctor. "There's a middle-aged woman, and then this young man"—his son—"who's kind of gross." Dr. Prini examined him, listening with interest, in case it was related to the ulcer. In extreme cases, ulcers can also affect the brain. Govi said that the young man was about five feet tall and that he tried to stay away from him because he smelled like nylon. He wore second-hand clothes from the Red Cross. "Generally speaking," he asked, "do they disinfect those?" And the woman had an indeterminate smell too, like a hospital smell. "Is it possible," he asked, "they have some disease that causes that smell?" This woman went around like she was in her own house, in Albania. In a way, it was handy having her there, since she made eggs or meatballs every day, most of which were for the young man. When there were extra, he ate some. The boy was a total pig—you know how Albanians are—and the woman too. They'd fill their plates with meatballs and stuff their faces with them; then they'd take a drink and scarf down some more. This process usually took about ten minutes, though sometimes longer because they would alternate meatballs and eggs. Govi managed to eat a few eggs, which actually weren't half bad. But the young man would give him dirty looks, and the woman would look at him like he was the pig. These two Albanians had taken over his house and turned it into a greasy spoon by day and a hotel by night. Especially because the woman slept in his bed. "Better her than that boy," he thought, even if he couldn't decide which of the two he found more revolting. The woman made a lot of noise when she slept, especially her breathing. He could also hear the young man's breathing from the other room, where he occupied the couch. It was like some kind of camp. But the problem was, exactly what was it that he had signed? Couldn't you perhaps inquire, discreetly of course?—he asked the doctor—Without letting on that I want to take it back? Actually, he wanted to ask the doctor: How long do Albanians stay—ballpark? Don't they have concentration camps for them? These Albanians, he said, were aggravating his ulcer, since now he ate nothing but fried food.

In addition, despite his young age, the son also developed a mild ulcer—perhaps it was genetic—and began not to recognize his parents. This is according to Dr. Prini. He'd wake up in the night, with no idea what time it was, and wander around the house with his stomach burning. In the adjacent room, he came upon two people sleeping in the same bed. He racked his brains trying to figure out who they could be. Then he went to look at them more closely and in the semi-darkness was able to make out a man and a woman. The man was snoring a little. He stood there staring at him, the woman too. He couldn't figure out how they'd got in. It was a mystery to him. They seemed like some married couple who had come to sleep in his house. Maybe a homeless couple or squatters. They were there during the day too. The woman was always in the kitchen frying something, he (the son) ate it, and she would fry up something else. Then the man, who was balding, would come and he would eat some too, especially if there were eggs, after which he would rub his stomach, saying he had indigestion. Since he often heard the man mention the far-off land of Albania, he assumed they were originally from there.

Dr. Prini is convinced that the root of this is the ulcer, a hereditary form that causes partial lipomnemonic cretinism (i.e., gaps in memory). He says that family members often don't recognize one another, without anyone ever acknowledging it. The root cause of all this is fried food, which is toxic to the body. Dr. Prini is writing an article on the subject to be published in the *Bulletin of Hygiene and Disease Prevention.*

PEZZENTI THE NOBLEMAN

He never laughed so as not to get wrinkles. He used a polish that kept his skin as taut and shiny as wax. When the polish dried it formed a sort of porcelain shell, which was beautiful to look at but extremely fragile. He couldn't make the slightest expression, neither of cheer nor surprise, or even chew, because he would start to crack and from the young man he appeared to be he would suddenly turn to shattered glass. He applied the polish around ten in the morning and once it was dry around eleven, he went out; and he could be seen strolling down the city streets with his beautiful motionless face. He just turned his head right or left and directed his eyes toward the window displays. Since so many people looked at him, especially salesgirls peeking out of stores, calling their coworkers to come and see, he thought that he caused a sensation owing to his smooth and youthful skin, which gleamed on sunny days. His morning outing served no other purpose than to sow admiration and amazement among the populace. At half-past noon his shell started to crinkle, but by then he was close to home, and he entered promptly because as far as he was concerned the show was over.

Once home, he removed the polish; it was like little scales in a color that suggested caramel; he picked them off with a fish knife. Underneath, his face was dull and sad; it seemed dusted in ash, not the face of a nobleman, but of an abandoned old man. In fact, he lived in an unsanitary cellar that no one else had ever entered. The plaster flaked off the walls and fell to the ground; he'd nudge it into the corner with his foot. He detested brooms so he never swept. Never had a more artificial man existed; he also had a wooden hand concealed with a glove. In his cellar, there was a metal cot and a dressing table. Instead of a bathroom in a corner there was a drop-off that communicated directly with the sewer. Rats likely came up from it on occasion, but that fact is secondary. He wore a topcoat indoors as a robe, since his house, being partly underground, was always winter temperature. He holed up in there all day long, yet you couldn't say he spent it thinking, because he wasn't inclined to thought, nor had it ever interested him. He was very handsome when he was young, they say, and vain. But he was admired as long as he didn't open his mouth, because then out came his voice, dull and insubstantial, a symbol of his impoverished mental state.

In the mid-afternoon he went to the soup kitchen dressed in rags; there he didn't have occasion to speak with anyone. He ate out of necessity, not enjoyment. Nobody knew it was the same person who could be seen strolling down the avenue at eleven-thirty. Many of the salesgirls even thought he was French. But he was just an eighty-six-year-old man.

He used the polish in order to look happy and to stand out a little from the local crowd and life. He wasn't an exhibitionist, as this description might seem to suggest; it was his way of living as a nobleman in a persistent state of youth. This polish is purchased by mail order; it's called Indurit and it restores the semblance of youth to the face, down to the collar. Actors use it when they appear on television or when they have pictures taken. It comes with a brush, like a polish; but it's an illusion, so no one uses it any more.

He also had a starched suit for his walk that he kept protected from the rubble and rats. There was a fake handkerchief sewn into the front pocket and a false collar in front. On his head he wore a synthetic toupee.

Then one morning he collapsed in the street; it was almost twelve-thirty. He was carried into a store and laid down. He smelled like a corpse and his face was in tatters. It was the many salesgirls from the shoe store who recognized him; but they kept their distance, owing to his odor as well as his startling face. His dentures had fallen in the street, as had his wooden hand; and under his jacket, when they unbuttoned it, were some rags bound together with an elastic. The paramedics from the ambulance studied his face up close, thinking it was a disease.

But it was the polish. It turned out that his name was Pezzenti, as in "pauper" or "nobody." No one knew him; he had no relations. He had a fake Monarchist Party card, purchased several years prior from some scam outfit, which gave him the title of nobleman. This information was gathered by the social worker before he expired at the hospital without a word.

CIMETTA THE PAINTER

The painter Cimetta, a native of Orte but resident of Orvieto, would paint lines when he was in a state of complete and total inspiration. They were very elementary lines, like those an illiterate would make, black and straight, without any appeal. This was all he painted.

He did a piece every so often, whenever he felt the need to express himself. In general he did them on a 30 × 30 wood panel. He said he had no preconceived idea when he sat down to work or any intention to make lines. He'd take the brush and voilà, the lines came out of him, but as if he had just discovered them at that moment. They were always the same lines, they didn't mean anything; but as he made them it was as if he was astonished by them, and he swore that they were his autobiography. An untrained eye couldn't distinguish one painting from another, and he couldn't distinguish them either; they were identical anyway. Nor did he know what each individual painting meant. As he painted it, though, he would say that it was a universe unto itself, so full of meanings that were so clear it was like he was writing a book, a book in installments about his life. But after half an hour he forgot what it meant, and with no painting did he ever remember.

A critic often came to visit him, Professor Guastalupi; he would sit in the armchair, look at the paintings, and say that there was a tenebrose element to them, yet it eluded analysis and therefore him as well. The "tenebrose element" was the sum of his critique; he considered it an important description, but couldn't say more. So he sat in the armchair and smoked as the painter Cimetta rummaged through his paintings to find one that was even slightly different. Generally they spoke little. Professor Guastalupi would stay there all afternoon and into the evening, sitting in the armchair trying to add something to his description, but nothing else ever came to him, which proved that his definition was complete, if inscrutable.

One day Cimetta worked up the courage to put on an exhibition. The first to arrive was Professor Guastalupi, who sat down in a chair. No one else came, and they both tired themselves out sitting and waiting. In the days that followed, the painter Cimetta regretted putting on the exhibit, and he did no more paintings for a very long time. Professor Guastalupi didn't come to visit, and the studio was left deserted. Once a client came looking for a landscape or still life or even an animal scene, on an 80 × 100 meter canvas. Cimetta went up to 30 × 30 at most, which the client deemed insufficient, despite not being picky about the subject.

Cimetta said that his paintings represented the tenebrose element, and seeing that the client, whose name was Del Ferro, didn't understand, he added that this element is found abundantly in nature, therefore also in still lifes, but only Professor Guastalupi could say what it was. The lines were never mentioned; he preferred not to use that word or any words that suggested it. The painter Cimetta said that, in conclusion, this was his biography. The client, this Del Ferro, repeated that he was looking for an 80 × 100 meter painting, and that 30 × 30 was too small. This is all that is known; then the painter Cimetta moved to another city, and if he kept painting he did so unbeknownst to the critics or Professor Guastalupi.

VICTIMS OF THE REVOLUTION

In the second year of the Republic, during the French Revolution, an artilleryman went to the Public Health Committee to propose his plan for a new cannon, which promised tremendous results.

A date was set to test it in Meudon, but Robespierre wrote the inventor a letter so effluent with praise that reading it struck him dumb as a stone. He had to be sent to Bicêtre in a complete state of idiocy, and as for the cannon, nothing further came of it.

This is reported in a medical treatise by Philippe Pinel, who talks about how during the Revolution there were often melancholics who thought their heads were filled with some heavy material, others who thought theirs were empty and shriveled like a nut. One melancholic believed his head had been cut off by a horrendous tyrant. To convince him this wasn't true, his doctor had a lead cap made for him and ordered him to wear it through the entire Revolution, so that the tremendous weight would prove to him that his head was still on his shoulders.

This issue of having a head led to many a supposition, back then. There was also a renowned watchmaker in Paris who thought his head had been cut off and then rolled off the scaffold like a cheese wheel, mixing in with the many others; and he believed that the judges, quickly regretting their harsh sentences, ordered all the heads to be gathered and returned to their proper bodies. But he was given someone else's head by mistake. The very idea disgusted him. "Look at my teeth," he kept saying. "Mine were so nice and now they're all full of cavities. Look at my mouth: it used to be healthy, now it's foul and diseased." Sometimes this watchmaker would sing and dance around his shop like his neck was unhinged; sometimes he became enraged over nothing and banged his head all over the place, trying to bash it in. He wandered around Paris searching for his original head and ran to all the executions to rummage through the basket where the heads were piled to see if his was there.

One day he ran into a colleague and they talked about the famous miracle of St. Denis, who walked along carrying his head and kissing it. The watchmaker ardently insisted that it was possible, that it wasn't a miracle, and gave himself as an example. At which the other one burst out laughing. "You debrained idiot—how could St. Denis kiss his own head? With his heels?" This unexpected reply disconcerted the watchmaker, who withdrew in confusion amidst teasing and laughter. He never mentioned the mixed-up head again; he dove into his trade with maximum care, but generally preferred to keep his mouth shut.

Pinel tells this story to demonstrate how sometimes logic is an effective cure for idiocy.

13

THE CARNIVAL OF '56

In 1956, on the evening of Fat Tuesday, in order to liven up the Carnival celebration for its employees, the city of Centanni distributed fake noses. This was the mayor and the youth assessor's idea. Nearly all the revelers put them on. But the most enthusiastic was a certain simple-minded Amadìo Cortellini, who put it on and didn't want to take it off. For the women, the city gave out hairy moles to stick on their faces or, as an alternative, fairy hats.

This Cortellini kept the nose on for days afterward out of some strange form of vanity. Until then, he'd been a regular, nice guy who lived with his elderly mother and looked after the chickens. There were forty of them. His mother had trained him when he was little and he made sure that they didn't get lost. He was able to collect the eggs, but he couldn't count them. Numbers were inconceivable to him. But he could recognize each individual hen and took them all into the yard to feed. He could also recognize if there were someone else's chickens and would shoo them away, as his mother had taught him, if they tried to sneak into the flock. He had no other particular inclinations, and once the chickens were in for the night he would go into town and sit with the regulars at the bar.

There was only one bar in town: Bar Nazionale, traditionally frequented by men. Cortellini started showing up there with his fake nose, held on with an elastic string. He was dressed the way idiots dress in the country, especially in times past. And upon seeing him everyone made some kind of remark, as one does at the sight of someone wearing a fake nose on a weekday. Cortellini always had his face scrunched up, as if he were laughing, but you couldn't tell whether he was laughing or that was his normal state. Everyone felt obliged to crack a few friendly jokes, what with the bar's lack of diversions, and mostly they were directed at the nose. But that was enough for Cortellini to get upset and start sniveling. "Have your fun but don't hurt the man," the barman said. Instead, the situation escalated, ending in the others trying to take the nose off, as would happen at any bar. But no one ever managed to get it, even though it was three against one. Even though they boxed his ears. He made a muffled "no" sound like a rabbit's grunt, and kicked backward pell-mell. "Keep back," someone said. "It's dangerous, he's out of control." The ones playing cards said that, because they were annoyed. At this point the barman said, "Cut it out," and left the bar to break them up. Then others too, who had been laughing until a moment before, said, "OK, enough's enough." It always got very close to a real brawl, because the two or three who had tried to take his nose away stopped joking around but were bothered by everyone's about-face, and the nose seemed expressly designed to antagonize them. This situation went on for months. The bar owner wanted to ban Cortellini from the premises; some considered this an injustice, saying he was a special case. There was constant debate until regional psychiatric services took an interest, at the mayor's behest. Someone at the bar had said it was irresponsible to give a fake nose to someone who's mentally disabled. Often the most pointed critiques of the city came from the bar. Psychiatric services went to examine him; there were two nurses and a doctor. The doctor said that the nose was dangerous on the symbolic level over the long term and it had to be removed. The nurses agreed, because even apart from the symbolic level, seeing him answer the doctor about that nose so smugly made them want to take it off of him. Therefore, they proceeded to the intervention phase. The doctor said, "Don't hurt him, because it could have repercussions on the symbolic level." The nurses said, "We know what we're doing, Doctor. It'll only take a second." But Cortellini had learned a very powerful nose-shielding technique at the bar; it involved kicking. The nurses were dripping sweat, and the doctor said, "Stop, we're in an advanced symbolic phase"; and to Cortellini, who was resting, they said, "Why do you like wearing that nose?" Cortellini made the same face he always does, screwed up and incomprehensible. Then the doctor said to the nurses under his breath, "I wouldn't want to provoke acute denial with overly direct questions . . ." So he asked, "What's your name?" "Cortellini." "And where do you live?" "On Via del Cantone." "At what number?" "At number six." To the nurses, softly: "There, see? We're getting through to him." To Cortellini, "Could you do something for me?" He stood there, saying neither yes nor no. To the nurses: "Now I'm going to test his conditioned reflexes . . . Hey, Cortellini, could I try the nose?" Cortellini said nothing. "Listen, now my two friends here are going to come over to see what it's made of . . . Go on, go on," the doctor whispered to the nurses. "I weakened his symbolic level." The nurses went over and reached out, trying to push his head down. Cortellini displayed incredible strength: he went rigid and bucked like a burro. The nurses tried to grab his foot, but one's finger got kicked and she got mad. The doctor said, "It's impossible. Can't you see? You're bringing out his negativity. Forget it." One nurse stopped; the one with the hurt finger clung to the hem of his pants, trying to trap his foot. "Forget it," the doctor said. "He's in the acute stage." After that, Cortellini shifted the nose back into place and said nothing, because he didn't remember what happened. This was the response from the psychiatric team, led by Dr. Motta.

The nose, made out of plastic-coated paper, lasted for several months, during which Cortellini was never seen without it. And this had some political repercussions, however improbable that may seem, because the mayor and youth assessor were charged with negligence in organizing the 1956 Carnival celebration for distributing fake noses without consulting the health department or regional psychiatric services about the risks. Indeed, when voting time came around they had fallen out of favor, and the health assessor was elected mayor.

Cortellini continued showing up at the bar with the fake nose, but since it had become a political issue no one tried to take it off him. For months he was seen by the ditch with the chickens, always wearing that fake nose. No one knows how it felt or whether it had some purpose. For example, if it had something to do with the chickens, as some people said at the bar. Because the chickens seemed to love him and see him as one of them, except more intelligent. Thus they obeyed him, not behaving anarchically, but also more or less intelligently. They respected the city ordinances regarding pasture, never entering private property or farmland unless Cortellini expressly led them. They were very orderly moving along the ditches and trails. If Cortellini lagged behind, they stopped to wait for him. And during the day they traveled kilometers through the valleys and fields. It was a good life, for them and for Cortellini, for example compared to chickens that were cooped up or fenced in. This is what people said at the bar, in discussions about the nose, which, however, remained unexplained. Even psychology offered no explanation for the phenomenon. The most Dr. Motta was able to say after examining him was that he was a simple man, subject to outbursts of rage and epileptic kicks.

The nose fell apart organically, almost without his noticing. His real nose had become whiter, but resembled the other. At the bar they examined it and discussed.

Yet among the things that happened during those months, there was a patron of the bar who, wanting to make fun of Cortellini, came to the bar one night wearing a fake nose. It was one of the leftover noses from Carnival. Thereafter followed a series of now-classic pranks, down to the cruelest one of giving him a 125-volt shock. The other fake-nose fellow was the ringleader of these amusements, and he found it so hilarious that he kept the nose on all the way home, and then for a while indoors with his wife and his children. One of the children had been born four months ago and had the downside of crying constantly, or at least quite often, turning family life, particularly at night, into agony. When he came into the house wearing the fake nose, the baby was crying and the wife was rocking him to get him to sleep. In the meantime, the soup was simmering on the stove and the wife kept yelling for someone to go give it a stir. The other son was playing a trumpet and kept saying "I'm going" without going, so the wife yelled louder, threatening him with a beating, first from her and then from his father. The little one, given this chaos, didn't fall asleep but shrieked, or resumed shrieking. This was the situation when the father came in with the fake nose; the older son stopped playing and ran up to him, ecstatic, and when the little one saw the father's face leaning over the cradle, was stunned into silence. So the wife ran to stir the soup. The little one waved his hands in the air toward the nose; he seemed enthralled. Meanwhile, the other son said, "Papa, Papa, can I try it?" But as soon as Papa took off the nose, the little one started to cry even harder. The wife abandoned the soup and ran over to calm him; the other son played the trumpet wearing the nose, and the boiling soup bubbled out of the pot. In this way they discovered that when the father wore the Carnival nose, the little one was calm and peace reigned over the family, like an inexplicable miracle. Thus the father was essentially obligated to wear the nose all the time, until the baby fell asleep, which took a very long time, but at least he wasn't screaming. If he woke up in the night all he needed was to see his father wearing the nose. He was undoubtedly a strange child, perhaps a psychoanalytic case. The father kept the nose ready on his nightstand and sometimes, even most of the time, forgot it was on. So the couple slept with her on one side, him on the other with his Carnival nose. It wasn't a pretty sight.

The wife came to think that maybe it wasn't a good idea and that the child might grow up to be different from everybody else. So they also consulted psychiatric services to ask whether a father wearing a Carnival nose could cause negative developmental effects. The developmental psychologist said that no such cases had ever come under their purview and they would need to run some tests. There was a speech pathologist in the group with an incredible nose. They showed it to the child but it had no effect; the baby didn't calm down, even though the speech pathologist got right in his face, just like his father usually did. The speech pathologist was Dr. Zecchi, and his nose was very prominent and unnatural looking. For a moment, the baby seemed confused. Dr. Zecchi put his nose in his hand for him to play with; he usually did this with children, it was one of his methods, because the nose is a powerful imaginative force, according to his theory, when given to infants as something to focus on or grasp. The baby screamed so loud that they had to call his father and pull Dr. Zecchi away, who didn't want to give up. In any case, it was a phase that eventually ended. Only the older son, growing up, remained somewhat close to his father.

And for the sake of completing the chronicle of events related to the Carnival of '56, it should be added that the fairy hats also had negative effects, probably because in Centanni no one had ever seen one up close. One young woman was so enraptured by them that she fell into apathy, as if she had caught a glimpse of another life and normal life was no longer worthwhile. All she talked about were fairy hats. She didn't know that they'd been distributed by the city; she thought they came from another world, and she waited years for the 1956 Carnival to recur. She used to be a waitress; then she became abulic and filthy. Her name was Rosa Pia Mantovani.

This episode was also used by the health assessor to remove the mayor. You don't just give people fairy hats without due precaution, he said at the city council, unless you're careless. Or incompetent. The mayor tried to respond, saying that the esteemed health assessor at that very Carnival, the 1956 Carnival, had come dressed as an archer. That too is careless, said the mayor, toward local institutions and health policy. "It pains me to remind you," the assessor retorted, "that the kind mayor, on that same occasion and from a position of great authority, gave a welcome speech wearing one of those fake Carnival noses, *and*," he added, "kept it on for the entire evening. Is that appropriate?" he asked. A councilman who was an ally of the mayor's said in his defense that since it was Carnival, the mayor had had a bit to drink that night. "Well not me," the health assessor said. "I was in complete control of my faculties. An assessor has to be clear-headed, that's what counts. A mayor even more so." A murmur went around the room, so he added that one can lucidly dress as an archer, or a cuirassier like the education assessor Mr. Zinani, or the Dottore (like councilman Leoni, mentioned along with many others, who all dressed on that Fat Tuesday as Indians or explorers along with their wives), which was completely different from putting on a fake nose under the effects of alcohol, with prejudice for political lucidity and the duties related to office. The lucidity argument was convincing, and everyone took the side of lucidity, even the athletics assessor, who had dressed as a pirate. The mayor was on his own, without a defense, trapped by the health assessor's logic. Whose name, by the way, was Ercole Prati.

The discussion was interesting because it revealed two opposing conceptions of politics. The heath assessor was a reader of Machiavelli; in particular, he had been reading his *Discourses on Livy* for years, and from there derived his political idea of lucidity. The former mayor, on the other hand, was self-taught.

14

COLLATERAL SUICIDES

In January 1981, a city sanitation worker jumped out of a window, falling onto a traffic policeman and killing him.

A butcher who wanted to shoot himself accidentally hit a contractor who was looking out the window across the way.

An out-of-work man whose wife had left him tried to crash his car into a building at a certain bend in the road, but the wall collapsed, killing a schoolteacher and wounding several children in the classroom.

On 9 June, a chicken seller, exasperated by taxes and determined to end things, lay down on the train tracks and stayed there for four hours. Until the train arrived, and trying to brake, derailed. A man on the train with a heart condition had an attack and died.

On 10 September, an alcoholic lawyer who'd lost everything jumped off a bridge. But along with him fell a pensioner who had tried to hold him back. The pensioner drowned, whereas the lawyer was taken to shore still drunk and unconscious.

PRIMO APPARUTI

What I'm about to tell you about Primo Apparuti is all true; he told it to me himself when he was in the asylum.

Primo Apparuti was a mechanic living in Nonantola in the Province of Modena. In 1918 he was voluntarily admitted to the insane asylum in Reggio Emilia. He said he couldn't stay out there anymore, he couldn't keep on this way. He was a bicycle mechanic and when he hammered on a piece of metal to reshape it he felt faint; he thought that the metal should complain and that it censured him with its silence. It made him feel so awful that tears came to his eyes and he ran to dunk the metal in water, hoping to alleviate the pain he had caused it. Half an hour would go by, and lacking the nerve to return to the metal, he would start mounting a wheel; but as soon as he tightened the bolts on the axle, the same voice inside reprimanded him, saying he was hurting the bolts and the axle. He had to stop. But seeing all the other bolts, he said he felt pained and distraught. He tried to resist, but a vice on his heart compelled him to loosen them. And after having loosened several, he felt he had to escape, and on his way out he apologized to the other bolts, saying he wasn't the one who had tightened them, and that if he loosened them the bicycle's owner would fall or even die. Through his tears, he could hear his children calling out, "Papa, Papa." So he closed the shop and posted a sign: "Mechanic deceased." Then he regretted having written it and giving customers a reason to feel sorry or upset; he went and took it down, without having the courage to look at the bicycles.

He often thought of killing himself, but he was assailed by the fear of being clumsy about it and damaging the furniture, or bothering people with his funeral. So he felt increasingly distraught, as if he had an indescribable weight on his heart, and it made him want to cut off his head, set it on his worktable, and beat it and yell at it until he wore himself out.

Once in a while, to vary the source of his affliction, he would go into the city and purchase a streetcar ticket for the last stop. But after a half kilometer or so he had to get off, having deemed himself unworthy of transport, and moreover, feeling like the engine was rebuking him. He started back down the street on foot, but when other streetcars loaded with people passed by, his heart tightened at seeing them subjected to that kind of force. He took on their pain, crying, and ran uphill after them promising revenge, cursing and mocking the passengers, and exhorting the engines to be patient, because later they would have joys the passengers couldn't even dream of.

Once he was beyond the city limits, he was placated by gazing at the telegraph poles, hugging and kissing them, measuring the distance between them, counting their wires, and in all this taking great comfort. He tried to imprint the shape and size of each one in his mind, and promised to come back and visit. These were the only moments of happiness in his life that he could recall.

THE REPUBLIC OF BORN IDIOTS

An idiot by the name of Sereno Bastuzzi lived in a barn. The barn was annexed to an abandoned farmhouse. Also living in the barn were Sereno Bastuzzi's father and mother, born idiots and farmers. Put otherwise, they lived self-sufficiently on a small plot of inherited land.

An idiot has a conception of agriculture all his own: he doesn't buy or sell anything; he doesn't use tractors or other farm equipment; he doesn't prune the plants or use chemical fertilizers, herbicides, or pesticides. He doesn't plant seeds, because he doesn't connect seeds with plants. An idiot considers others stupid and laughs when he sees someone throwing grain on the dirt. In fact, he'll decide to go peck at it like a chicken. By nature the idiot doesn't eat meat; and in fact the Bastuzzi family did not—they ate eggs, chicory, and other greens like chicory, or directly related to it. Their diet is based on chicory and they notice it first in the field and with joy. Meanwhile they don't care for nettles and instinctively trample them, and thus in places where an idiot or a family of idiots live there are very few nettles. The idiot does it in spite, not to rationally eliminate a weed from the garden. They do the same with brambles, similarly a cause for complaint and retaliation.

The case of the Bastuzzi family has been studied in order to determine the type of agriculture adopted by an idiot or a community of idiots left to their own devices, based on the hypothesis that eventually they will be the last ones left in the world. The study was conducted by Dr. Consolini at the University of Pavia from 1960–61, with the collaboration of his assistant Dr. Maria Stanca.

A single idiot requires at least six hectares of land to live on. One part is wooded and another cultivated as a garden, with a stream running through or at least a spring with potable water. In the summer, the idiot stays outside in the shade of the trees, preferably by the stream, and only exposes himself to sunshine for agricultural purposes. He likes being near chickens, with which he has an affinity. When a rooster finds an ear of wheat or a worm on the ground, and with his particular cluck calls the hens to eat, the idiot runs over too, and is often the first to eat. He also likes being near cows, which are fond of idiots; and if they see one lying outside on the grass, they go beside him and follow suit. It seems that cows can distinguish idiots from the sane, and while they fear the latter owing to their manias, feel utterly at ease with the former. In fact, the Bastuzzis had four cows (and a young bull) and they all lived in peaceful harmony;

the cows ate the grass, the idiots the chicory; they also drank natural, whole milk together with the calves. To a cow, there's no difference between an idiot and a calf. The idiot also becomes very skilled at finding eggs, far surpassing the skill of the hen hiding them. Once in a while, though, they miss a few, thereby perpetuating the chicken species.

Chickens that belong to an idiot die of natural causes, i.e., of old age; something that is never observed among civil populations, where chickens are always killed and cooked. The Bastuzzi family wasn't in the habit of cooking them because they did not know fire. When a chicken senses it's dying, it distances itself from the flock, going to the edge of the Bastuzzi property, and hides in a ditch or a thorny bush and sits in silence. The cows also go to die at the property line, in a patchy spot where no one passes because the soil is loose.

If an animal wanders off Bastuzzi land, usually the neighboring farmers throw rocks at it, or chase it away with a stick. Therefore, it quickly learns the perimeter exactly as recorded in the land registry. The Bastuzzis attained a sense of their territory in the same way and don't dare leave it. Sereno Bastuzzi often walks along the property line with a trail of cows and chickens in tow, looking askance at the neighbors with their rational, intensive farming, and all their toil to improve the terrain. The Bastuzzis, on the other hand, never make any effort and never seem worried about a season's progress from the agricultural point of view. This is cause for anger among the neighbors.

In summer, idiots gain weight; in winter, you could say they go into hibernation or semi-hibernation. In the summer, the Bastuzzis wake up with the sun and go out to the trees to eat wild fruit. In the meantime, chicken, turkeys, ducks, and cows graze down below. They don't respect lunch- or dinnertimes. They drink water with great gusto. Sereno Bastuzzi seems to savor it intensely; his eyes half-close and he swishes it around in his mouth like a liqueur. He probably relishes its coolness on hot July and August days. This kind of pleasure is not seen in cows, which are more gluttonous; yet it is noted among chickens and birds in general.

Dr. Consolini in his office says that the Bastuzzis stay in the old barn in winter, and when the days are very short and gray they're always asleep. Dr. Stanca notes that they snore intermittently. Once in a while one of them will get up and grope around for some walnuts or hazelnuts, or dig up carrots in the old garden. They would never dirty the straw with manure. They are also accustomed to clothes, mostly wool coats passed down by their forebears. They may also eat snow. But in winter they don't laugh; they move slowly and vacantly like sleepwalkers, then return to the straw. The entire countryside is asleep in winter, buried in fog and ice. The cows eat the tree bark and hedges that they refused in summer. Everyone loses weight, even the geese and chickens. Some die, the more fragile of them. This too is cause for anger among the neighbors, i.e., the fact that the chickens are left to fend for themselves rather than being killed. This undermines the foundations of agricultural society and attracts chickens from other coops. The neighbors claim that the Bastuzzis are a danger to farming, and set a bad example for their children, who believe that they live in a republic and that the Bastuzzis are republicans, not idiots. When, for example, a little boy runs away from home because he fought with his father and spends a day with the Bastuzzis, he comes back home with a libertarian mindset, much like the mentality of bovines or farm birds; in other words, conceiving only of the fleeting present and underestimating his father.

The hibernation phase can last up to three months (in rare cases, up to four) for the Bastuzzis; from this Dr. Consolini concludes that idiots in their natural state would not be able to survive above the arctic circle or in altitudes higher than one thousand and two hundred meters. The Bastuzzis live in the province of Cuneo, with an isothermal line of five degrees centigrade in January. If it falls below that temperature, idiots lack sufficient corporeal and arboreal reserves to last the winter. Dr. Consolini therefore places the ideal isotherm for the natural settlements of idiots even farther south, yet in a climate with high precipitation, or at least two thousand millimeters of rain per year. Favorable locations he cites are Grosseto and environs, or the southerly piedmont regions, like Bassano del Grappa or Massa Carrara.

Heat, on the other hand, is tolerated by idiots up to extremely high temperatures, over forty degrees centigrade, as long as drinking fountains are not scarce; otherwise the heat is too dehydrating and leaves the idiot parched. Dr. Stanca confirms this data in her study on idiot adaptability in North Africa and Africa. This study earned her a university chair in 1964.

If everyone in the world was an idiot, Dr. Consolini concludes, the human race would never go extinct. Its numbers would reduce globally and it would inhabit the more temperate or warmer latitudes, as in Dr. Stanca's study; the world's forests would replenish. Cities would disappear as population centers and the ozone would return to the atmosphere. Humans are herbivores by nature, Dr. Consolini states, and in fact the idiot spontaneously and voluntarily eats plants and tree fruit; he can be found alongside herds of herbivores, which recognize him and with which he mates. He also occasionally mates with fowl. Incidentally, it has also been noted that the chickens at the Bastuzzis' have begun to fly.

THE WOMAN, OR THE WHALE

A fat woman by the name of Paola Parletta occasionally had bad diarrhea. She would sweat on the toilet all night while outside a storm raged. She got diarrhea every time the thunder clapped and the sky rumbled, especially on summer nights, with strong winds and twisters. Her body was very fat and there were pimples on her face, but she was convinced she was thin or looked thin because of her tiny head and rather petite cranium. As she sweated on the toilet and the storm raged, she thought that someone must have put a laxative in her food. It was the only idea her tiny brain managed to squeeze out, and even if she strained it couldn't produce a more substantial one. This idea came to her in August 1955. And so she spent the whole night between abdominal spasms, fear of the thunder, and feelings of resentment, even toward people long out of her life but who flashed through her mind as possible culprits who had come expressly to poison her even from great distances, sneaking into the kitchen when she was out and slipping out without a sound. She spent the rest of her life bitter and suspicious, always trying to catch someone with a laxative in their hand, pouring it into her soup. She suspected her neighbors; she'd run into them several times on the stairs carrying packages; she also suspected one of her brothers who perhaps wanted to thus inherit her estate, i.e., her bed and mattress. Sometimes the water from the aqueduct tasted a bit unusual, so she was suspicious of that too, but she'd never caught anyone in the act, even though she watched the faucet for hours to see if anyone ever tampered with it.

Thus her life revolved around these bouts of diarrhea and all of her mental activity involved it. Up to the age of thirty-six she complained after every episode, attacking and haranguing suspects; she'd rampage around the house in her robe, her face pale from abdominal pain, but her body still ample and bulky. She would suddenly go up to a relative or friend and ask, "Who put the laxatives in the soup?" It was to catch them in the act, or at least make it known that she wasn't some simpleton or easy target. Then she started making threats, hurling abuse at all purgative and laxative administrators, who also included hypothetical accomplices working nervously in the shadows with an eyedropper.

Then, with age, the diarrhea became more regular and independent of atmospheric disturbances or cold spells; it would come on every two or three weeks, no matter what the weather or season. But it did not stop being the number one problem of her existence.

This Paola Parletta, who remained a Miss even as an old woman, then tried a different tack. Since 1960, she had gotten even fatter and her head proportionately even more microscopic, and she suffered from shortness of breath and heart palpitations. She'd prowl around in the morning, not talking so as not to wear herself out, and tried to be clever, digging through the trash for the vial that had contained the laxative, rummaging through the medicine chest or under the bed, always in silence, because her heart couldn't take shouting or confrontation. Sometimes she found a few drops of liquid on the floor, in the kitchen, but said nothing; she would wait until they were bigger, or on the tablecloth or next to her plate. She was suspicious of the salt as well.

Then one day she fell off the toilet and dislocated her hip. After that, she remained sitting in a chair raving about her meals and the two-faces who took care of her. That was her life. Nothing else happened to her.

THE MARTYR TO FEET

Dr. Dialisi's real life began at a well-advanced age, and it all started with a pair of shoes. They were leather oxfords. He'd bought them one day virtually without trying them on, in 1937, at age sixty-two; he said that on seeing them in the window he felt inspired. They turned out to be so narrow and stiff that wearing them was torture. He wore them from morning to night anyway, even keeping them on until it was time for bed. The idea was to stretch and soften them with use. But the shoes never stretched and his feet continued to suffer. What happened, though, was that whereas he used to be a man without any interests or desires, from then on he became a man who thought of nothing but his shoes. No one around him suspected his suffering because he kept it hidden. One only noticed a cautious step, like someone walking on eggshells, and a focused, in a sense more spiritual, look on his face. In the meantime—this was 1938—his feet had been rubbed raw, there were bony growths on his heels, and in spots they had started oozing pus. They were a painful sight. But rarely did he remove the shoes. He only freed his feet at night, stretching them out on the bed and looking at them. He wouldn't hear of turning to the cobbler. He and his shoes had formed a symbiosis devoted entirely to ravaging his feet.

Dr. Dialisi (a widower) had a daughter named Veronica. She, upon seeing the change in her father, who no longer spoke and walked a great deal with a worsening limp, thought she would take him to an orthopedist. It must be said that Dr. Dialisi had developed certain general ideas about humanity and predestination: we were given heads to think—he would say—mouths to breathe; arms and hands to touch and grasp objects; legs, theoretically, to walk; and feet, so tender and exposed, were given to us to keep pride, envy, and lust at bay—otherwise we would have hooves, like horses. He said this to the orthopedist, during his appointment. The orthopedist was quite struck, as he was used to considering feet differently, as an anatomical fact, not a spiritual one.

After a while, Dr. Dialisi intensified his persecution further: he would goad dogs into biting his feet; he would let them be trampled by school kids or wherever there was a crowd; once his foot was pierced by the tip of an umbrella without his uttering a word of complaint. He compared them to the ribs of Our Lord, but without intending blasphemy; in fact, he didn't have a low opinion of feet as is common—to him, they represented the core of his moral life. In any case they had formed two abscesses that were so extensive and deep that they quickly brought him to his grave. Antibiotics didn't exist yet; they were invented a few years later. With antibiotics, he might have been saved. In his final days, he didn't allow anyone to examine his feet. He had grown so weak that he couldn't stay standing. Everyone begged him to at least take off his shoes, but he wanted to keep them on even in bed, and he smiled at the orthopedist talking to him at his bedside. When he lost consciousness his shoes were removed, but were immediately put back on, as the clinical picture was quite extraordinary, and at that point there was no more to be done; the orthopedist was of the same opinion.

If anyone had determined what this religion was that Dr. Dialisi believed in, there would have been converts, because his death was a beautiful death—the death of a saint. In total, his ordeal lasted three years. When he expired it was 1940, and World War II was already under way.

CESARE LOMBROSO

As everyone knows, Cesare Lombroso was a scholar specifically of criminals and deviants (including idiots and artists), characterized by corresponding defects of uncertain origin. Thus in 1881 Lombroso conducted a study of musicians and their geographical distribution in relation to volcanoes and volcanic soil. He found that at the time there were exactly 1,210 musicians in Italy, 650 in Germany, 405 in France, and 239 in Austria-Hungary. Then followed Belgium with 98 musicians, Spain with 62, and last came Sweden (9), Ireland (7), and Holland, with a total of one. Based on this data, Lombroso states, no conclusions can be made, neither as to the determining influence of climate nor that of volcanoes. Meanwhile, the distribution of musicians in Italy was heavily concentrated in the major cities as opposed to the countryside, forests, and marshes, where musicians are rather scarce. Of the cities, Naples had 216 musicians, Rome 127, Venice 124, Milan 95, Bologna 91, Florence 70, Turin only 27. Evidently the marine element takes precedence; in second place, hills, and in third, volcanoes.

Ethnic composition, however, is unclear. In painting, cities also prevail, followed by hills; at the bottom are L'Aquila and Syracuse with one painter each, and Bari, Grosseto, Sondrio, Porto Maurizio, and Teramo, with none. Sculpture and architecture show more or less the same results. Towns that produced no or few artists had been afflicted with malaria or goiter. However revealing these figures may seem, as Lombroso tells us, they are to be taken with great caution, especially concerning the primacy of cities over climate and volcanoes: indeed, individuals often pass themselves off as natives of a major city even though they moved there as newborns or children from their tiny villages off in the swamplands or lava beds.

Besides climate, meteorological events also influence artistic impulses and all criminal expression in general. The highest instance of violent acts (as well as strong poetic and artistic inspiration) takes place around the first-quarter moon, when there are also atmospheric disturbances and storms. A full moon with clear skies brings about stupidity and the impulse to flee. The last quarter makes the criminal and the artist more rational and human, and more apt to report others and be repentant. Still others can sense meteorological variations two or three days before they occur, and by their degree of agitation indicate whether the weather will clear up or remain turbulent. In Milan, in 1871, one could observe a thief, typically calm, cursing profusely in the hours before a strong wind. And if the wind came with rain and snow, the swearing was depraved and obscene, in an astonishingly precise scale that could predict the upcoming weather, including storms and floods.

Revolutions, too, as expressions of criminality, are very much affected by climate. In a text from 1887, Lombroso shows that the highest number of revolutions in the ancient world took place in July, and the least in November. Rome and Byzantium, out of 88 revolutions, had 11 in April and 10 in March, June, July, and August. From this data, it is clear that more revolutions broke out in warm months than in cold.

In the Middle Ages, revolutions were staged midsummer; subsequently, from 1550 to 1791, we find 10 in spring, 14 in summer, 3 in autumn, and 4 in winter. From 1791 to 1880 there were 495 revolutions in Europe, 283 in America, 33 in Asia, 20 in Africa, and 5 in Oceania. Regarding Asia and Africa, the most were in July; in Europe, in July and March; in the Spanish-American republics, in January, which is the warmest month. And evident in all this, says Lombroso, is the exclusive predominance of the thermal factor. In fact, the number of revolutions increased from North to South, just as the heat increases from North to South; we see Greece coming in with 95 revolutions, i.e., the most; and .08 Russia, the least; we see smaller numbers in the Nordic regions, England and Scotland, Germany, Poland, Sweden, Norway, and Denmark; the greatest in the southern regions: Portugal,

Spain, European Turkey, southern and central Italy, and a medium number in the central regions. A notable exception is Ireland, which shows an unexpected number of revolutions for its geographical position. But it must be noted that the climate in Ireland is greatly softened by the beneficial warmth of the Gulf Stream. The Gulf Stream has had a corresponding effect on art and artistic movements over the course of the centuries.

But Lombroso is famous particularly for measuring criminals and he had started to measure artists. In 1872 the measurements of criminals were the following: arsonists prove to be the tallest at 1.71 meters; murderers follow at 1.70. Then come thieves and burglars, 1.69 meters. The lowest average height is found among rapists and swindlers, between 1.65 and 1.66 meters. As regards body weight, it corresponds to the rule of stature almost exactly: very low weight among those who commit burglary and robbery, at 61 kilograms, and rapists are even lighter, 57 kilograms. Burglars and murderers are good-sized and hearty, while forgers and rapists show a higher number of lightweights, and it should also be noted that out of 8 crimes of rape, 10 of forgery, and 13 of arson, generally 5 are committed by hunchbacks. On the other hand, you find only 3 hunchbacks out of over 250 burglaries and murders, which for Lombroso confirms the negative opinion regarding maliciousness and lust that people have always had of hunchbacks. As for the head, the largest craniums are found among forgers, slanderers, and swindlers; burglars come right after, differing little from murderers, then thieves and rapists. The smallest is found in arsonists, who often have ultra-minuscule heads and non-existent brains. Taking height into account as well, the arsonist type therefore comes closer than any other to the conventional idiot, if you exclude the case of hunchbacked arsonists.

Cesare Lombroso was born in 1835 and died in 1909. At a certain point in his life he went to Russia to exchange ideas with Leo Tolstoy, the famous writer, and to study him if possible. But Tolstoy refused to see him, saying that his theories were the theories of an idiot. When this was referred back to him, Lombroso was highly offended; he challenged Tolstoy to prove it statistically. But he received no reply. This took place in 1897.

INCONCLUSIVE APPARITION OF THE MADONNA

The first apparition that Adele Bagnoli saw took place on 14 May. So said the expert who examined her. In the days prior no change had been noticed in the girl, who was in her usual good mood, eating well and sleeping soundly. Her father, aged fifty, was a watchman at the telegraph office. She knew how to read and write, and when she told the story, she seemed very sincere. Her mother, Maria Capanni, was a calm woman and said she'd never noticed anything particular about Adele; for example, she didn't sleepwalk or have convulsions. She'd had a bad cough since she was little. And her two other daughters had died of diphtheria. Seen together, the sisters looked a bit anemic.

The apparition occurred in a place called the Pianello, one kilometer away from the Bagnoli residence. It was an isolated place, without any houses. In the lower part were lush chestnut trees; higher up, scattered ferns and junipers. It was flat on top, with a slight dip, and among the lower shrubs there was a juniper at least a meter and a half tall, and this is where the Madonna appeared to Adele. Note that there were no crosses, no poles with icons of the Virgin, no votive tablets or tabernacles, nor any legends or superstitions at all connected to that place. The closest sanctuary was on the road to Castelnuovo, devoted to Our Lady of the Cough (i.e., Health).

That 14 May was a Friday. Adele, after coming home from school, had gone out that afternoon to take the sheep to pasture. She took a friend along, thirteen-year-old Emma Giovannelli, who was blonde and smart. They passed the time playing with a rubber ball. Then after leaving the sheep up in the mountains, they chased the ball down into a field surrounded by grapevines, owned by Emma's father, who caught sight of them and yelled at them not to trample the grass and to go tend the sheep. They ran off, and Giovannelli kept yelling at them not to cross the field but to go around. But it was no use; they raced to the hedge and jumped over, first Adele, then Emma behind her. The juniper was twenty meters away, and when Adele looked up in the middle of it she saw a girl about her size, pretty and blonde, dressed in white. So she stopped, a little surprised, and said, "Emma, look, a little girl." Emma didn't see anything and asked, "Where?" and wanted to keep going up the mountain to go and call the sheep. But Adele said there was this girl looking at her, and she turned to look at her if she moved, and kept shaking her hands as if calling to her. A little scared, Emma shouted: "Watch out, it's the devil!" So Adele got scared too, and both took off running. Up on the mountaintop she felt her knees start to buckle and she'd gone pale white.

Thus she was brought home shaking by her sister Enrichetta, who was fifteen and happened to be out in the field. At home she didn't want to say anything, and at dinner she wouldn't eat. She seemed ill; but even before, she was that way sometimes by nature. After being asked what was wrong several times, she told her mother that she had seen a little girl at the Pianello; she wasn't scary and was very pretty; but she ran away. That night she wasn't able to sleep.

The next day, which was Saturday, when her father returned and learned of this, he forbade her not only to go the Pianello, but even to discuss the occurrence. So for the whole week she didn't go back. But the neighbors were already talking about the appearance and saying that Adele had seen a little girl above Giovannelli's field, where the juniper was; and one woman exclaimed: "It must be the Madonna." So from that moment on everyone said that on Friday at the Pianello the Madonna had appeared to Adele. Who meanwhile had become even more withdrawn; she went to school reluctantly and barely said a word. This according to her mother and her teacher.

On 23 May, a Sunday, to show her it was nothing and she should get over her melancholy, her sister Enrichetta took her up the hill. But as soon as Adele spotted the juniper she saw the little girl dressed in white, her hands folded over her chest. Once again they got scared and ran down into the field, but on the opposite side, where there was a little hamlet called Burano. A few people gathered, and they all started talking. They said that it was the Virgin, and that by now everybody knew it; but they said there needed to be proof. And everyone, including Adele, who was a little hesitant, returned in procession. As usual, just past the hedge, she saw the same little girl in the same spot as before, with her arms outstretched. Everyone said you're supposed to ask questions right away, and they suggested many to her and pushed her ahead to ask them, until she, conquering her fear, asked: "Who are you?" Then she said that the reply was: "Maria Concetta." Everyone was awed and excited, and drew back a little in respect. Then they continued with other questions: "Will we be happy? When are we going to die? Is it going to rain today? Who stole my ring? When will my son come back from the service?" And many other questions of various sorts, to which Adele, after relaying them, would reply: "Yes, no, today, tomorrow, in a month, etc.," or she'd say that Maria Concetta had said nothing. Everyone was thrilled.

That night at home Adele still didn't want to eat and just stared blankly. The next day, her father, hearing the talk going around, decided to go up to the Pianello with his daughter and a friend and try it out. They arrived and there was Maria Concetta, above the juniper, almost as if she had been waiting for Adele.

"You see her?" they asked Adele.

"Yes," she replied. "I do."

So to test her they wrote a few words on a piece of paper, thinking that if it were really the Madonna, she would be able to guess anything. They give Adele the folded-up piece of paper and told her to ask: "What is on this paper?"

The response was: "Three words."

It was true. They were dumbstruck.

Thus began and went on for weeks a continuous procession of people coming from all the nearby towns to visit the juniper. They left ex-votos, planted crosses, and the priest had already put down a box to collect offerings; he too wrote notes, folded them, and waited for her to guess. He said that it wasn't actually the Virgin, but at the very least it was some holy spirit. And Adele, who at first had been afraid, now always wanted to go back to the Pianello; and she asked questions of Maria Concetta, who replied or said nothing.

Once they asked how long she would be on the juniper to talk.

She replied: "Until 23 July."

"And then," they asked, "will you come back?"

Reply: "Yes, after two hundred days."

Question: "And then what month will it be?"

Answer: "February."

They counted, and it was true. It was one of the occurrences that impressed them the most. Then they wanted to know how many churches there are in Rome. And Maria Concetta, via Adele's mouth, said: "Ninety-five parishes." Everyone nodded in astonishment, and the priest also said that was correct. Thus every day it was constant interrogation. An old man who lived in a house on the state road came forward. "Ask Maria Concetta if she knows what my name is." Adele asked and then said, "Filippi." And upon hearing his name, exclaimed contentedly, "It's true!" And he looked around as if to say, D'ya hear that? But everyone objected, saying that question didn't count, because everyone knew his surname. In these cases the priest said, "Enough! Don't tire her!" or "One at a time," if there was a big crowd. Or: "Such questions are not permitted," because they wanted to know about matters of jealousy or personal interest; what their wife was doing, what their husband had done, and even worse things and gossip. And he didn't want them to ask lottery numbers either. "That is not appropriate," he said. "It would be disrespectful." He, however, asked, "Who among us will be saved?" And after relaying and listening, she replied, "Angelo Acerbi, of Bruciata," which is a hamlet at the turn for Castelnuovo. Everyone was even more astonished, because no one would have ever thought of Angelo Acerbi, a forty-year-old man, who worked in the fields and sat at the cafe like everyone else. And they also asked: "What's in my pocket? What color is my handkerchief?" She would reply, "It's turquoise" or

"It's checkered." Thus arose discussions to interpret these responses.

At home, Adele did nothing; she didn't help, didn't study, and could barely say her prayers. She was fixated on returning to the juniper; she would have stayed there all day. She said that the Madonna appeared as a little girl, with a pink face and the expression of someone always about to laugh. Black eyes, shoulder-length blonde hair, and a tulle veil. A white satin dress, with a starched, full skirt; her feet could not be seen. She looked around and her lips moved when she spoke, with the clear voice of a young woman. Adele could see her from any distance, even from the top of the opposite hill—over two hundred meters, as the crow flies. But the apparition was clearest at about three meters from the juniper; if she came closer, the apparition receded, and at about a meter's distance, it vanished. If she stepped back again it would reappear, smiling and serene.

An employee from the telegraph company, an acquaintance of her father's, wanted to go with Adele one day. He went next to the juniper and reached out, asking: "Is she this big?" Adele replied that he was touching her head; she was one and a third meters from the ground. Then as he lowered his arm little by little, Adele said: "You're touching her neck, her chest, her waist, her hips, etc." She said that his hand was always in front. If Adele went around the juniper, the Madonna rotated on her axis, always presenting her face. She couldn't tell if it was transparent or not. A few times she saw a small light on the branches, or a sort of very bright dot. The priest said it could be the Holy Spirit.

Then it also happened that, toward the end of Our Lady's stay on the juniper, the matter attracted the interest of the schoolteacher, Mrs. Brevini. After hearing so much about it, and seeing Adele, distracted and inattentive, fall behind in her studies, she wanted to come up with her to the Pianello and figure out if there was anything positive and instructive to it or if it was just a waste of time. It was early afternoon, and people were beginning to pour in. The teacher asked the main world capitals; then the heights of mountains; the longest rivers; then she reviewed history. And up to that point she was very pleased. Then she asked for the seven times table, and Maria Concetta recited it to Adele without one error. Then the nines table and elevens, and then the twenty-fours. The crowd, circled around, said: "Wow, she knows everything"; or "It's the Madonna prompting her." For her part, the teacher was quite satisfied too. Then she said: "Let's try some division," and gave her two four-digit numbers, so there was already a certain admiration from the start, and the most pious and religious women whispered that it was a miracle. And when Adele replied, some people fell to their knees; many fans applauded, and the teacher was moved. Then it happened that an ignorant illiterate came forward and asked what five plus zero was. Adele consulted with Maria Concetta and replied: "It's six." Everyone looked at the teacher, who scowled; in the end the illiterate was turned away; he'd gotten the response he deserved.

And the arithmetic problems continued. There were so many people that they extended all the way up to the top of the mountain and many were spread out over Giovannelli's field. If an answer was not exact, it was always very close or close.

A month had gone by since the first appearance. By now people pointed Adele out, and even when she was on the street some asked her their fate. But there were also skeptics, who ran behind her booing, and said that she belonged in the madhouse. The skeptics said that Adele had an uncle who chased the sheep and read out loud to them. He went by the name of Don Giovanni Fabiano, and he liked to dress up as a priest. They often made him sing in church; he ate nothing but fruit. Some said he wasn't crazy though; in fact, he had a very good memory. But the skeptics saw it as a flaw.

These matters made Adele feel ashamed; she had crying spells and didn't want to leave the house. Apparently she went to the Pianello by herself a few times, crossing the woods at night.

So in conclusion, to bring all this fuss to a halt, and also perhaps owing to certain illicit traffic, the authorities intervened, and had the juniper cut down and taken away. And they ordered Adele to stay home for a while and the local doctor to examine her. Some strange legends went around for a while afterward; that some crippled and blind had been healed, many kilometers away; that out of the cut stump had come blood as a voice said "Santificetur." And it seemed that some inexplicable phrases were heard as well; the priest said it was Latin.

It even seemed that the juniper with its last bit of voice had spoken a name, a certain Torricelli, who lived in the lowest house down in the valley. The town watch said that a hiss could be heard coming out of the trunk, and at a certain point a distinct "Egidio Torricelli." When he was notified, Egidio Torricelli was quite taken aback; he said he knew nothing about it.

NEAR SUICIDES

After a series of vocal cracks in March of 1982, a tenor locked himself in his dressing room and shot himself with a revolver. When they broke down the door he was alive because the gun was a prop gun. The tenor stated he hadn't known.

A pacifist lit himself on fire in the street; but he immediately regretted it and jumped into a fountain. Subsequently, he would say that he saved a human life.

In October, a lonely aging psychologist decided to kill himself with sleeping pills; but during the wait, he decided he had suffered a mental breakdown and requested an emergency stomach pump.

After lunch, a forty-three-year-old man had the bad habit of keeping a wedge of apple in his mouth and rolling it around with his tongue. His mother would say, "swallow that, quit acting stupid." He pretended to swallow it but secretly kept it in. One day in November, his mother, after telling him repeatedly to "swallow that apple," smacked him on the back of the head. The apple went down his throat and got stuck. Nothing helped, no matter how much they hit his back, and he choked to death. Thus the news that he committed suicide because of his unsubstantial, drab life is false.

SUNDAY DRIVES

The Bassanini family was composed of the family head, his wife, and three small children. They were a normal family, except when they were in the car. This happened on Sundays for their so-called Sunday drives, which they'd done regularly since Bassanini had bought the car. Bassanini drove at moderate speed, always ready to brake as needed. His wife helped him spot dangers in the distance. But when they came to a fork in the road, with a sign saying, for example, right for Genoa, left for Livorno, drama ensued. Bassanini, with a line of cars behind him and unable to stop, went blank and lost all sense of right and left. The children yelled, "Papa, Papa, go that way!" and his wife said, "Be careful, Gino, this is dangerous; go right, the other way is for Livorno." It was a matter of seconds; a commotion and chaos broke out in the car; he clutched the steering wheel; if he hit the brakes they started honking behind him, and in hesitation at the last instant he would wind up awkwardly on the grass or in the bushes, or with a wheel or two in the ditch. As long as he went very slowly, the accident was never serious. A few times his fender hit the Livorno–Genoa sign. And the cars didn't help but instead yelled out the window "jerk," or honked to mean "jerk." But sometimes, with all those cars on his tail, he didn't register either Genoa or Livorno and turned directly onto the wrong road. What happened was this: in order not to forget he kept saying "Livorno," "Livorno," to himself, and then some sort of enemy impulse inevitably made him turn toward Genoa. The children shouted, "Papa, turn around," and the wife, too, "Turn around." But behind him he had a line of cars that were also on their Sunday drives and he couldn't stop. He moved as far to the right as possible. Slowing down to the right, he scraped against the guardrail, and the children yelled, "Papa!" clutching his seat. This sometimes went on as long as ten kilometers. Until Bassanini's nerves got the better of him and he veered off the road. He never had a real accident. Some bangs and bumps, culminating with his children's and wife's screams. After that they were all relieved. The wife would say, "That went well," and they'd push the car to a point where they could turn. The worst were the crossroads without anywhere to stop to think and calm down, and he had to make a decision and handle the wheel at the same time, leaving the whole family tense and scared. The father said he went blank because of all the responsibility weighing on him, and because everyone was counting on him. Fortunately forks of that sort were rare. On straight roads he was confident and drove in accordance with the road signs.

The day afterward, the children, who were in elementary school, wrote their in-class compositions about their nice, quiet outing, and that their father smoked as he drove. In truth, Bassanini had to stop periodically to smoke because he couldn't smoke and drive at the same time; he said that cigarettes interfered with maneuvering, for example if a curve suddenly came along; but even going straight, if he thought about smoking, he couldn't keep his mind on the road. So every once in a while to break the tension he'd stop on the shoulder and have a cigarette. Sometimes his wife smoked too, and the children played in the backseat.

The era of Sunday drives ended when the car ended, taken away by the tow truck. The family always remembered the automobile era as an era of great excitement, echoed on Mondays in the children's compositions, always a little sugar-coated, in keeping with scholastic tradition.

Bassanini never felt like buying a second automobile. He said he'd gotten used to the control panel of the other one and was too old to learn a new one from scratch.

THE FAILED WHORE

Her name was Rosa Maria Bianconeri and she lived on a small piazza called San Giovannino in the village of Caliceto. When she looked out the window she often saw dogs or a tired, thin horse passing by. People sent them to send her messages like, for example, she was an animal. The dogs were sent by a neighbor, Bàssoli, a contractor, who lured them there by scattering meatballs on the ground. The horse belonged to General Ciuschi, and it passed by on occasion when the dogs didn't suffice. Hearing hoofbeats, she raced to the window, and they made it parade in front of her all whipped and rundown, to insult her. They probably ganged up on her because she was never interested, neither in Bàssoli nor in General Ciuschi, when they pursued her on the street or secretly made kissing or sucking sounds at her. There was also another she'd never even spoken to, but who maybe had wanted to marry her. Actually not maybe: certainly. And now for revenge, he amused himself by sending signals of his offense. He purposely went through the piazza making a wide rowing gesture, purposely looking away from her window and door; she saw him through the shutters, and immediately flew into a rage, because he was trying to call her an "oar," as in "big fat oar." So she threw open the shutters and spit in the street to say, "You! You're the scoundrel and the animal." But she was so agitated and enraged by the insults of this Paterlini that her mouth went dry and she could barely spit anything except a wad of paper—she was used to passing her days chewing on paper, especially blotting paper, chewing it into little balls. So she spit these little balls but they didn't go very far, in fact they fell straight down and stuck to the ground below the window, until someone passed by and stepped on them or kicked them away, to show her that she'd always be down and out.

Then there was also a certain Panzieri whom she'd known since she was a little girl because he harassed her with vulgar propositions, yet always from very far away so that she couldn't hear; but she understood, and she heard him breathing heavily when he went by, like someone pretending to have asthma. To avenge himself, or just to vent, he'd grown a goatee and went around with it curled into a little hook. In particular, one time she was sewing at the window. She heard someone walking down the street and she looked outside. There was Panzieri coming from the right with his goatee as usual curled into a point to provoke her. He sauntered with all his arrogance and his little goatee jutting out, by which he meant to say, "failed whore"; i.e., a hooker who didn't hook. And in fact right in front of her at the window he stopped with Paterlini, who was coming from the other direction, and they shook hands. With this conjunction, they intended to make a complete sentence with a verb, as in: "Big fat oars are failed whores." At which she yelled through the shutter slats a string of words to say "stop, enough," i.e., she yelled, "Copiers!" and "Ravers!" (because they were unoriginal and raving mad). This wasn't just any insult, but a phrase that was supposed to cut them to the core. But the two shook hands again to repeat the sentence with the verb addressed at her, i.e., to again call her a fat oar and failed whore, and she yelled some more, this time to strike down to their souls, screaming: "You two are archaic!" i.e., just like Noah's ark, full of crap. From this it was evident that she was very smart whereas they were a couple of bums. In fact, they left immediately. Paterlini strolled slowly as if rowing and Panzieri stroked his beard as if in a house of ill repute.

Men were very interested in her, they always had been, and so by that point there was an agreement to insult her and call her a whore, or big fat whore, in every possible way. One group passed by just to tell her she was fat. They suggested she shouldn't eat because she's bursting, or indicated that she's a cracked barrel, pointing at her rear end. Many would go out of their way to come and tell her; she'd see one from the window where she was always sitting overlooking the piazza while she sewed or strung beads. That was the job she did for a company, the Deanna clothing company. Still others passed by to tell her she was skinny. At first she thought they were friends coming by purposely to counter the others. Then she saw that they said "skinny" in such a way that it really meant "fat." For example, one of them carried a walking stick, but one day she noticed he was shaking his head to mean "no," i.e., "You're no stick." And then he hit a tin can with the stick and kicked it away, as if to say, old containers end up in the trash, "You toxic old fish"; toxic because old tin causes tetanus, and old fish because there were still bits of spoiled tuna in the can. They thought she didn't understand, but she had a very sharp mind that understood everything, even more than they did.

Once in a while trained chickens passed by, also sent to taunt her. They were tall, skinny chickens that look more like boiled chickens; Mrs. Prati often followed behind. Once she also saw a slightly flat rubber ball coming slowly from the right. She couldn't say where from exactly. The ball stopped in middle of her field of vision, against a step; and she didn't see anyone. The ball was there for the entire afternoon, and this was also an expression intended to mock her. At that point she couldn't take it anymore and she started making personal comments very loudly about these gimmicks of the deflated ball and chickens, which demonstrated that she had the keen intellect of a deep thinker. Since she lived on the third floor, she had to yell very loud to be heard all the way down in the street. But she had a polyp in her vocal chords that, if she raised her voice, would alter it and take away its sound, so that she yelled with pure breath. She'd gotten the polyp from drinking tap water; in fact, the aqueduct was controlled by a certain Dr. Milanesi who'd been at war with her for eleven years, ever since she stopped receiving him, and he sent her seawater full of flukes and polyps small enough to pass through a colander or cheesecloth. This was demonstrated by the fact that she could feel them tickling her throat all the way down when she drank, and as soon as she raised her voice in the slightest they took it away; but Milanesi didn't come around because he wanted her to be the one to go looking for him, at the aqueduct offices where he worked and where he had some scam papers to make her sign registering her as an official whore instead of as Mrs. Prati.

What's more, there was the matter of Mr. Contento. Mr. Contento came over from the Deanna clothing company on the twentieth of every month, always saying kind words; then he took her finished work and gave her some more. While Mr. Contento was there, the others often sent dogs into the courtyard to bark, and she would flush with shame. Then by the time Mr. Contento was gone, the courtyard was littered with trash and vegetable scraps left there to disparage her. Once there was even a handyman outside banging around the whole time Mr. Contento was there, about half an hour. You could hear him pounding and drilling; and she grew increasingly ashamed. Then the handyman continued even after, using his tools with sexual gestures. The people passing by laughed, or stifled laughter, or without letting him see, imitated her and Mr. Contento as he checked her buttonholes and complimented them. This happened every month; sometimes even during the night, especially the dogs, which came all the way up the stairs and wiped their paws on her doormat. According to her, the dogs were definitely sent by Panerari and he incited them to bark, because she was always behind the curtains across the way sewing and looking out, and then he'd throw bones out the window. Vegetables too. This had been going on for eight years and had reached this point: Mr. Contento rang her bell and immediately someone else rang upstairs; or they kept the radio on full blast playing a cheesy love song. If not the radio, it was the television. She couldn't take the broom and bang the ceiling in Mr. Contento's presence and so she pretended not to understand the insinuation, as did Mr. Contento. But all this skewed whatever she said, so that she would say "no" when she meant "yes" and get confused; and she didn't catch Mr. Contento's comments about her stitching or his praise of her as a seamstress. As soon as Mr. Contento left and the door closed behind him, she ran to get the broom and banged the ceiling like a madwoman. But they kept playing love songs at full blast so they could be heard down in the street, where Panerari had sent the dogs running, and whoever passed by tugged on his beard to say: "failed whore"—to her instead of Ms. Panerari or Mrs. Prati! At night they all sang little ditties about her and Mr. Contento on their honeymoon. The lyrics were indirect, but she would wake up and understand. In fact, she'd wake up just in time to see someone passing by with a slimy stride, like a slug. This happened regularly before the twentieth of the month, when Mr. Contento came from the company.

MEMORIES OF CONCENTRATION CAMP SURVIVORS

In Pescarolo, at the mouth of the Po, there's the case of a male individual who was a prisoner during the last world war at the concentration camp in Mauthausen for about two years. But he says he never noticed, because at that time Mauthausen wasn't yet well known and famous. Only after the war did they find out that everyone had been starving.

They served this gruel that you couldn't actually tell if it was soup or porridge, but he says they gave it out for free. This was novel to him, and he accepted it without comment. So he would eat his gruel with gusto. Sometimes he thought he could detect a hint of beans. He was very thin when he went in, since everybody in Pescarolo has been thin for ages, as it's such an underdeveloped area. The other people in the concentration camp were thin too. He didn't know where they were from, so he thought it was just a general attribute of the population. That is, it didn't seem to him that they ate so badly, as was demonstrated after the war. Some people complained at the time, but he thought it was a matter of character. Or someone would suddenly get a craving for chicken and go on and on about it. Chicken, as was revealed after the war, wasn't served in any of the concentration camps; that is, it was practically unheard of as a potentially edible animal. They also said afterward that it was freezing at Mauthausen, but he had truly never noticed, because winters are colder in Pescarolo. Pescarolo is a town without a single economic resource; every so often the inhabitants catch some fish, but the fish are thin, starving. The people are therefore used to it and don't worry much about their standard of living. There are a few chickens, but they've got rickets; they're fed fish bones and only occasionally lay eggs. But the eggs are practically empty; they don't contain any substantial nourishment. Children eat the shells, but they don't develop much.

One day he happened to be riding his bicycle from Pescarolo to Comacchio, pedaling very slowly, when a jeep filled with soldiers pulled up next to him. And they were so insistent, he says, that he had to get in and leave his bike there, unattended. Then they loaded him on a train with a bunch of other people. They hardly spoke. He expressed his worry for his bike, which had been thrown carelessly in the ditch. He asked: "Will I ever find it again?" But nobody wanted to talk. All the way to Germany. World War II was in progress: this, too, was discovered later. At the time it mainly seemed like there was widespread incivility, even among the railwaymen, who pushed and shoved and made no effort to be understood. But at no point during the trip was he asked for his ticket. For his part, he couldn't forget his bicycle, abandoned in a ditch. You could say that in his two years at the concentration camp this was his suffering. He even had nightmares about it, the spokes and chain rusting, or someone slashing the tires. He wrote letters home: "Everything's fine here, how's it going there? Have you found my bike?" But he never got a reply. He tried to talk to the guards about it: "I used to have this bike. Would it be possible to notify the police station in Comacchio by telegram?" These were lengthy phrases that they didn't have the patience to stand there and listen to. He never did find his bicycle. Who knows what happened to it?

THE POET DINO CAMPANA

A certain Melegari was born in Marradi, the hometown of Dino Campana, the famous poet; this Melegari attended the University of Bologna from 1970 to 1974. During oral exams he always found a way to mention or bring the discussion around to Marradi so that the professor would immediately perk up and say, "Marradi, the hometown of Dino Campana." After this the professor would present a few anecdotes about Dino Campana, usually how he lost the manuscript of *Canti Orfici*, or his travels on foot, or the fact that Campana wasn't studied enough in school. If the professor was female, the comments had to do with the relationship between Campana and Sibilla Aleramo, the famous writer. At that point, when the professor (female or male) had finished speaking, Melegari added that since he was also born in Marradi, he had a great-uncle who had seen Dino Campana in real life; in fact he used to see him on the street every day and knew what street he lived on. At that the professor would get excited and say that Campana was a misanthropic poet, quite unapproachable. In general he avoided people, the professor said, and even at the Caffè delle Giubbe Rosse in Florence, where both the Futurists and the Vociani poets liked to go, he on the contrary kept to himself in the corner. This was the point that appealed to all teachers indiscriminately—that is, that Campana kept to himself in the corner. The female teachers liked to say that Campana looked like a bum, and despite this Sibilla Aleramo loved him passionately. At that point they were well into the exam, at least halfway through, and the professor was more than satisfied with themselves and with Melegari. It was the word "Marradi" that exercised an irresistible power over professors, and there had never been one who didn't succumb to its allure. Mentioning it at the end gave the entire examan air of originality, and the rest of the material no longer really mattered, or rather had become mundane and academic, something to gloss over, whether it was literature or something else like geography.

One characteristic of the female professors—not all of them, but the ones who weren't married—was to say that Sibilla Aleramo's name was actually Rina Faccio. By this they probably meant to say that as a poet she wasn't quite as valuable as people thought, and that talking about her was more of a favor to her than the other way around. Likewise, it was Dino Campana who did Sibilla Aleramo a favor with their tempestuous love. Thus with these professors you had to pay Sibilla Aleramo little attention and appear skeptical at both her real name and her pen name. Yet there were others who placed enormous import on her; in that case, you had to look excited and interested, and they'd handle all the talking. In fact, these professors were just waiting to hear the name Sibilla Aleramo so they could start talking; Dino Campana was merely a preamble, as was the town of Marradi. But in one way or another, Marradi got the entire department excited. That was the truth. And Melegardi exploited it for his academic career, without ever needing to read the poems of the poet Dino Campana directly.

When he was still a student, once in a while Melegari would be asked to substitute at the middle school. These jobs usually lasted a week, and since there was always a Dino Campana poem in the textbook, he had the students do a summary in class, then he'd say that his uncle had been friends with Dino Campana, who was now dead, whereas his uncle was alive and therefore a living witness. And he said that Dino Campana seemed like a poet even when he was young, as early as middle school, when everyone threw rocks at him. His uncle, however, defended him, because he was a great poet. As an adult, he had a very thick mustache, it was his distinguishing characteristic, as well as his hair, as the photographs attest. He didn't bring up Sibilla Aleramo because kids at that age aren't very mature. Then he would have them read Dino Campana's biography in the textbook; this was the second or third day of his substitute job. The biography was usually about ten sentences; he would supplement it with a few anecdotes from his exams, like for example that all his poems had been lost—because of the Futurists, he told the class. But he rewrote all of them, verbatim. Then he had them close their books and he would ask: "Where was Dino Campana born?" and give an 8 out of 10 to whoever answered. Whoever got it wrong had to copy out the biography at home and do a geographical report on Marradi. When he went into the teachers' lounge his colleagues said, "Nice, you're doing Dino Campana." No one knew much about him, though they knew he was born in Marradi, even the math and gym teachers, and the priest who taught religion. It was universal knowledge throughout the school system. At this point he would say, "I'm from Marradi too," and he claimed that the entire room perked up, and the female literature teachers already had the name Sibilla Aleramo on their tongues, some to reveal that her name was actually Rina Faccio, others to allude to the tempestuous love between the two poets.

This Melegari finished his degree in 1974 with a thesis on Dino Campana; but he bought it already written from a student who made his living writing theses for other people. This student's name was Pignèdoli and he never graduated because every time he did his own thesis he ended up selling it. Either because he needed the money, or because he gave in to the demands of graduating students who knew he was weak and tormented him until he sold it to them.

When Melegari appeared before the graduation committee, there was a professor who immediately started in with the lost manuscript of the *Canti Orfici*, and another added that the Futurists were always hanging out at the Caffè delle Giubbe Rosse and most importantly so was Giovanni Papini, the famous critic, while Campana was off by himself. Then since there was a female professor among them, Sibilla Aleramo came up; at which another female professor on the opposite end of the committee piped up to call Sibilla Aleramo by her real name, Rina Faccio; this professor had never been married, unlike the other who had mentioned the couple's tempestuous love. Then came the moment to mention Marradi; indeed, Melegari mentioned it, and owing to his extensive experience cut with it, added that he was born there. This fact won him favor with the committee, so that when his uncle came up as an eyewitness, his thesis was highly commended and the president said in his estimation they had heard enough. All the professors declared their agreement; therefore, Melegari passed and graduated.

Melegari later resold this thesis, and it was redefended many other times as a final thesis, even in other cities where there was a flourishing market for university theses. Even if by then no one knew that Pignèdoli had written it, this thesis on Dino Campana became so renowned among students, because it earned unanimous approval from the male professors and divided the female professors into two factions, that the candidate barely had to open his mouth and the committee members would duel it out; something that inevitably happened when Sibilla Aleramo was brought up under her real name Rina Faccio.

Every once in a while in Italy you come across someone who graduated with a thesis on Dino Campana; that person will, if prodded, talk about the Caffè delle Giubbe Rosse and how Campana was a misanthropic poet. Melegari also belongs to this category, with the bonus of having been born in Marradi and having had an eyewitness uncle. These two characteristics make him special, out of all the graduating students specializing in Dino Campana.

DOUBLES AND DWARVES

In an old treatise on dwarves and fools it says that the jester of King James IV of Scotland was a double being, or in other words, a Siamese twin. Of the two individuals that composed him, one was full of intelligence and charm and was a good musician, and his handsomeness and wit enchanted the ladies at court. The other, on the contrary, was clumsy, an idiot and a drunk, to the point that he ended up killing his brother, later dying himself from alcoholism. These two half beings never got along in life; they beat each other and were constantly grabbing bottles from one another's hand: one to drink it, the other to throw it away.

In the same treatise on fools, Sir Grenville Temple recounts that in 1835 during his trip to Tunis he was introduced to an extraordinary character; it was a dwarf named Abu Zadek; he was just shy of sixty centimeters tall. He was forty-five years old and had four sons and four daughters; and a wife who was, they say, extremely beautiful. Sidì Mustafà, during his travels, had seen him and brought him to Tunis, giving him a magnificent apartment and magnificent clothes, and having him entertain the entire court. Every once in a while they put him in a jar of preserves, and when there were visitors, the bey's brother told them he had just received some candied fruit from Costantinopolis, urging the visitors to open the jar and take some. As soon as they put a hand on the jar, Abu Zabek would jump out, to the great fright of the guests, who couldn't stop repeating in terror, "Allah! Allah!"

THE DEVIL AND THE IDIOT

The peculiar thing about Nereo Zaghini was that he was afraid of traffic; he said that someone hiding in traffic was going around trying to hit him; he said it was the devil who had come just for him. Sometimes he saw him biking through an intersection, but always very far away, like at the end of the street, and in any case passing by never turned to look at him. He said this was likely a sign of the devil.

He could tell it was the devil because he wore a plaid coat that flapped in the wind and nondescript pants; but he had to squint very hard to be sure, because he always appeared and disappeared very far away on the horizon. The devil seemingly took no notice of him, although in fact he was seeking him out. He could suddenly materialize behind him and mow him down. Therefore he avoided open spaces, like squares or big streets or the suburbs around Milan, so he wouldn't be exposed; it was the only precaution he took, not because it was useful, but mainly so as not to have any reason to blame himself should any sort of collision ever happen. Once he saw him on a bike flying down a hill; he couldn't be sure it was the devil himself, but said it was likely. The coat flapped and seemed plaid. Plus he was moving so quickly and recklessly that he said to himself, "Now that's the devil." Indeed, he vanished at the crossroads. He was also careful at traffic lights, because since the devil had no respect for anything, let alone rules of the road, red was more dangerous than green, and in fact he'd heard of pedestrians hit at an intersection, even on the sidewalk, in the leg or side, and knocked down. The cyclist often fell too, but got out of it limping away and leaving his dented, blown-out bike behind, so that it seemed stolen, as it actually must have been.

One winter in 1970, when he didn't yet have this fear and wasn't unemployed, an unidentified man on a bicycle knocked him down and sped off without a word, without looking back. It didn't seem like a regular accident; it was as if the cyclist had purposely sought him out and targeted him, and that he had actually been after him for some time. Yet he'd only bumped him, which was lucky indeed: one step forward and he'd have hit him right in the chest. He could have died, busted his ribs, or broken his spine. A small piece of reflective plastic from the pedal had fallen on the ground. Zaghini picked it up and kept it; it was proof, for lack of anything better. After that, Zaghini read the local news very carefully; or rather, the only thing that interested him in the newspaper, which were the traffic and accident reports. Certain details led him to determine whether an accident was caused by reckless driving and true diabolical madness: for example, if it involved a hill and someone who'd been seen barreling down without applying the brakes or sounding the horn. And other similar cases, for example where the devil completely defied the right-of-way and became a danger to the public, going the wrong way down a one-way street or turning in a no-turn lane or not slowing down over a speed bump or in a gutter. Sometimes they included the harebrain's full name, but that didn't mean anything—it's easy to make up names and give false information, especially to journalists who write passively without even realizing the meaning of what they write.

To tell the truth, he'd never seen the devil closer than a kilometer away, and always in a flash like a bolt on a bike. If the devil had appeared to him close up, and on foot, he might not have even recognized him. Yet he often found metal balls on the ground, and said they must have been lost by the devil; or bike parts, usually small things like broken plastic from the taillight, nuts without bolts, a brake cable, a brake, little springs, often ball bearings. And all this was the devil who had lost them from riding so fast. He found collar buttons too, but those weren't proof of the devil's presence, and so he tossed them away after a moment's scrutiny to make sure they didn't arouse suspicion.

Anyway, according to him the devil had never managed to find him since, and that's why he rode so quickly without noticing the bolts on the bicycle or the condition of the car. In fact, since 15 August 1974, he kept finding auto transmission belts, valve gaskets, oil stains, radiator caps, hoses, and all kinds of bolts from the engine block or the chassis. Indeed, if the devil wasn't on a bike, he thought he saw him in old, ridiculous jalopies, all banged up and rusty, decades old, with punctured tailpipes, and driven at top speed. Maybe souped up.—That would be why he found little parts on the street. They were parts that came off the engine, sometimes unimportant parts, but they suggested that the devil had been left stranded and the engine had overheated. More than once he'd seen black smoke from a car in the distance and smelled burnt rubber. All signs that the devil, hot on his trail, driving like a total madman in complete disregard of all road signs, and the car's engine burned out or crashed, after which he abandoned the car and got back on his bike or into the first car he found. In fact there were lots of cars on the side of the road, completely filthy and full of shoes, cigarette butts and ash, with "car dead" written on them to say that the car wouldn't start. The cars were parked badly, with a tire or two up on the curb, so that even from a distance you could tell they'd been parked by the devil. It wasn't uncommon for them to have a flat. Every week Zaghini went to the junkyard and asked the worker Donnola where each car had been picked up; he'd look inside and usually it was a horrendous sight, from the dirty, grimy upholstery littered with hairpins, to the engine that had been driven into the ground and was useless. Once in a while there was a car that was brand new but all its oil had burned up so the whole engine needed to be replaced. If there were cigarette butts in the ashtray, candy wrappers, dirty socks, old newspapers, etc., it was a sign that the devil had probably used it for one of his joyrides.

By all accounts Zaghini was a good man. He wasn't contentious, didn't have a temper, and would have been a good worker if this thing about the devil speeding madly through Milan traffic hadn't always kept him distracted, always a little out of it, like a person who keeps thinking little funny things and laughs to himself instead of keeping his eye on the cutter. Zaghini lost a lot of time on all this surveillance and investigation to gather evidence, this painstaking scrutiny of news reports, just as other people spend on sports or hobbies; and he would say that this was his hobby, except you needed good instincts and a versatile mind to do it. In other words, it wasn't a hobby for everyone. In any case, the devil was really a secondary issue, he said in confidence, and a very private one, with no bearing on a working man's life, and seeing as his sightings always took place rather far away, at most he smelled something burning or heard metal clanging or a crash, or spotted a rickety bike whizzing by for a couple seconds. If he recounted all this, he'd laugh as if it were nonsense; and he'd laugh about the particulars, the sheer amount of lost objects. Which, for his own amusement, he collected and displayed, in a case that said: "The Devil's Loose Screws."

Nonetheless, Nereo Zaghini wasn't always so good-humored and tolerant when it came to the devil, also because he constantly read about poor defenseless creatures getting hit, and widows, and people who were already disabled, and dogs. The devil certainly didn't mean to do it; he wasn't interested in people, or dogs, or broken bones, or damage to motor vehicles and traffic lights in general. In that sense, the devil was a perfect idiot, an asocial dimwit. And the authorities didn't notice. A traffic officer was even hit in an intersection and knocked off his platform. There was talk of a car with a brake malfunction spinning out, whereas there was no doubt it was the devil and his ignorance of road rules. On this occasion the devil appeared in the press as a resident on Via Trento e Trieste by the name Locatello. It was right there in the paper. The press was full of idiots; the authorities likewise had acted like idiots in this matter, especially the traffic police; and above all, the devil was an unqualifiable idiot, who had probably even forgotten the original purpose of his haste, to hit Nereo Zaghini, whom he had chased at breakneck speed from the beginning; he'd probably forgotten that name entirely, and all that was left were habit and an insatiable hunger for pure speed.

This general idiocy and insensitivity owing to which traffic had become a senseless hazard for everyone had plunged Zaghini into a state of worry, in which he didn't laugh so much. He felt responsible, for many if not all of the road accidents, responsible even if not legally culpable, because ultimately he had been the one who set the devil in motion. The devil has a different way of pursuing each person. Most people don't notice; they think it's chance. Whereas he had noticed because of the mistake the devil made on his bike, when he'd just brushed past him dangerously. Except now this private persecution had become a serious public hazard.

Since the month of March 1979, after he became unemployed and thus had more time to spare, he'd started directing traffic, first standing on the side of the road making imperceptible gestures; then motioning with a paddle and a sash on his coat sleeve. He mostly helped people cross the street, especially women carrying groceries and children leaving school. He checked that there wasn't some madman or imbecile driving up, or rather, he checked that the devil wasn't popping out in the distance, perhaps ignoring the red light and crosswalk. The paddle was for him to have official gear and not look like a troublemaker or someone with an addled brain. The paddle served to earn him the trust of the public, who generally believe in paddles and badges. Indeed, no one ever found out any of this. Everyone thought he was authorized by the city, because he carried out his job responsibly there on the corner of Via Adua and Via Mezzofanti, maybe just a bit anxiously, asking pedestrians to move quickly and egging them on. In any case, he had little authority over the cars, which always ignored him.

Well, one day he suddenly saw someone on a racing bike, in racing gear, with a plaid shirt or something quite like it. He saw him when he was still very far in the distance, pedaling down Via Mezzofanti all hunched over. You could tell he wasn't a racer, not even a responsible individual aware of the dangers of the city and its intersections. Based on this, he most likely had brakes that didn't work or were about to give out. There was a crosswalk, and the pedestrians were about to cross. No one had noticed the bicycle, which still seemed very far away, nor had they noticed its abnormal speed and the fact that bit by bit it was surely losing parts, like pieces of the back brakes. This occurrence was neither certain nor confirmed, but it was highly likely. It was but an instant for Nereo Zaghini. The pedestrians were on the opposite side. Zaghini held up his paddle and rushed across at a red light to stop the pedestrians in time, thinking he would be able to save himself too. Just then a car came from the left and hit him.

The devil was no idiot and above all he wasn't in as much of a hurry as he seemed. He had managed to wait for years (by then Zaghini was sixty-four), and then came to take him, by car. Nereo Zaghini was the idiot, not looking both ways before crossing the street. This is more or less what was said to the paramedic in the ambulance; on the basis of which, the driver, one Angelo Ciuschi of Melegnano, was acquitted of the charge of second-degree manslaughter.

STAR-CROSSED SUICIDES

A certain Marietta, married and unhappy, had a lover who was unhappy and married too. Their respective unhappiness was principally due to character and not solely to the tribulations of their relationships. In fact, they would meet specifically to weep together and lament their sorrows. The lover, who was called Paride Germi, promised her that they would kill themselves one day, in a hotel, and this Marietta (née Nosèi) would clutch him, crying, and say, "Promise me." And Paride Germi would reply, "I promise." Note that if they had been of a different temperament they could have gone on being normal, or at least semi-normal, lovers. But they rejoiced in bad fortune just as others rejoice in good.

Thus they agreed to meet at the Hotel Regina on Via Makallè at ten in the morning. Paride Germi had a revolver. Most likely he intended to shoot Marietta and then shoot himself on the bed beside her. But the first shot, as the police later determined, was fired prematurely and, unfortunately, punctured his leg. Then he shot Marietta, who was pleading with him and sobbing. But the pistol was old and the shot misfired. The bullets dated back to the First World War; they were nine caliber military leftovers, and you could clearly see that the brass had oxidized. Paride Germi later stated that the aforementioned Marietta had kissed his hand with "desperate force" and begged him to kill her. As it was an automatic pistol, he had to cock it, but he was crying so much he couldn't see and Marietta was so insistent and sobbing so much that another shot accidentally went off, this time going through his shoe and foot. This one really made him suffer, whereas he'd barely felt the first shot in the thigh. People started knocking at the door, since the two gunshots had made such a racket. Paride Germi replied, with impressive calm, that he had heard them too. Marietta implored, "End it," along with mad declarations of love. Paride Germi was on the verge of fainting, especially at the sight of his shoe filled with blood. But the gun went off again; Germi says he didn't know much about weapons, he'd never handled one before, and that the revolver was extremely sensitive and had something wrong with the trigger. Furthermore, his hands were shaky by that point. The bullet went through the wall and shattered the mirror in the adjacent room, where the guest started screaming for help. Before the concierge—and the bellboy, and the security guard, Silvio Mèsoli—broke down the door, Paride Germi managed to shoot the gun one last time, aiming more calmly and carefully. But he says he couldn't see at all, and was delirious; so instead of hitting Marietta in the chest, the bullet went through the wall again. After that, he was immobilized and disarmed. He put up no resistance. He voluntarily handed over the revolver, which still had two bullets.

He was convicted of attempted homicide with extenuating circumstances and lost the use of his foot. This happened in Genoa on 6 October 1950, and it is a famous case.

BATTISTA THE PINHEAD

On 4 September 1868, a newborn was left on the foundling wheel at the clinic in Voghera. His tiny head was immediately an object of wonder. He was given the name Battista.

Battista was an abnormal subject, or a microcephalic idiot, without memory or intellect. He had thin, delicate skin, and his forehead, cheeks, limbs, and neck were covered in a very fine down; his forehead was receded and sharply angled, and there was a fold on his crown so prominent it formed a crest. He walked by skipping with his back hunched and his hands swinging; he didn't sit, but crouched on the ground, and he was extraordinarily prone to jumping, so that if you offered him a finger he would hop up and grab it; if he saw a cane he would cling to it like a true quadrumane. From the ground he would jump up on the tables and the armrests where he would balance, wobbling without falling over, and moving his head like a monkey. When he went to eat he would smell the food, as he smelled any object offered to him.

As he grew up, his head became proportionately smaller. The down on his face disappeared, and his movements were also less simian. He still hopped, but no longer did he climb up people's backs and crouch on their shoulders as he did in his early years. Now, if you contradicted him, he would yell, stomp his feet, and curse. They had managed, in other words, to bring him a little closer to the human type.

He learned the names of almost all objects, and for many of the others, if he didn't know their name, he could communicate their use by gesture. He was very transported by music, and if he found himself in a hall where an orchestra was playing, he would rush over, following along in great excitement and laughing at the music of each instrument. Then he would imitate the players' movements and copy the sounds with his voice and mouth. He was afraid of larger animals, but he loved monkeys, although even if domesticated they rejected and threatened him. He believed that thunder was a very bad man, and so was very frightened of it; when he heard it he wanted the door closed so it couldn't get in; as soon as it subsided, he would say it was sleeping, and seemed relieved and content. When he heard chickens squawking in the yard, he got upset because he thought they were saying bad things about him.

When he was sent to a school for the mentally deficient, he created such havoc that they returned him. He did learn how to count to three. But from then on he became more vain: he would pretend sign with a twig, and pretend read, even upside down, uttering indeterminate words. He always wanted his little book, and he thumbed the pages, projecting a certain seriousness. He flew off the handle if anyone touched it and hid it in a secret drawer.

It's no exaggeration to assert that Battista was one of the most renowned pinheads in the world. Professor Tamburini brought him to the university and presented him to students as a model idiot. Also, many foreigners traveling through Italy came specifically to admire him. Nonetheless, in class, Tamburini claimed that it wasn't facial angles that made the idiot, for Battista's showed an incline of sixty-eight degrees, the same as the poet Ugo Foscolo's.

One memorable episode took place in 1899, when Giosuè Carducci, another poet, visited the clinic. It was 30 April, and having seen Battista many times as a famous case in pathology treatises, he wanted to meet him. Battista jumped right into his arms, as if he recognized him. And all were witness to this strange juxtaposition: Giosuè Carducci, with his big stately imposing head, benevolently stroking Battista's tiny one, patting the crest as he would with a brother. Battista, however, only said a certain obscenity, and then repeated rhythmically and contentedly an insulting, mildly vulgar word, which is a synonym for idiot or thick-headed. Carducci didn't take offense at this, because he'd been told that it was his usual way of expressing happiness, given his rather small vocabulary.

Since then, however, for no apparent reason, Battista could be seen standing motionless and silent, listening to music, almost a bit sad; whereas it made him extremely irritated to be told he smelled.

THE REALIST WRITER

There was once a fellow who considered himself a realist writer. Thus he wrote everything that happened to him. His name was Vincenzo, but in his novel he appeared under the name Ernesto. Everything he did, he did with the intention of writing it. For example, he would sit and stare at the ceiling, so he wrote on the page: *Suddenly, Ernesto sat down and stared at the ceiling.* Then, not having much else to say, he stuck his finger in his nose. But he didn't write that. If at all, he would write it in a more artistic form. For example: *Ernesto passes the time lost in thought.* That meant he was sitting at the table with his finger up his nose. Sometimes he would sit like that for an hour. He called this a stalled phase in which there were no salient happenings to report. At most he would write that Ernesto couldn't gather his thoughts. In truth, while waiting, when he wasn't picking his nose, he was picking his ear. But that was not a novel-worthy event, not even for a realist novel such as his. These are details that get left out of literature, like using a fingernail as a toothpick. So he stood up and then wrote: *Suddenly, Ernesto stood.* He used "suddenly" to give the novel a sense of drama. However, once he was standing, the novel was stalled again. He couldn't sit back down lest he fall into repetition, so he went out and wrote that Ernesto had gone out.

His was a novel of facts. He'd already thought of the title: it would be called *Ernesto*. And the book jacket would say "realist novel," lest he be confused with the intimist writers who just talk about minor details and illness, and ponder what life is or what the novel is.

He roamed the streets and faithfully reported in his notebook that he was roaming the streets. He wrote: *Ernesto roves the city*. This was an example of his style. Then he went into a cafe and he wrote that he had gone into a cafe and that, for example, he was sitting at a table smoking. He found smoking at the cafe to be very realist. And he added that the cafe was very smoky and crowded, but that he was off by himself. But this was no way to make progress with the novel. He had begun around nine in the morning, when he had sat down and set about staring at the ceiling. By noon he'd written half a page, more or less. It'll be a novella, he thought, sitting at the cafe; meanwhile, he stuck his finger back up his nose and released the air in his gut. He didn't write that either, though; instead he wrote that Ernesto snuffed out his cigarette and took a swig of beer. This was a sentence he liked, but it barely took up a line. Beer went along with the novel, though after two or three he would get distracted and forget to take notes. For example, at this point he unintentionally got caught up in conversation, which led to another two or three beers, and then two or three more. And he had the impression that now many, many things were happening in such rapid succession that he didn't have enough time to write them down. Actually, he stopped thinking about it, he just thought about the company and the beer. And he probably made some clever remarks that would have been brilliant in any novel. He also made public bets that made everyone laugh, and the whole cafe played along. In other words, he created the realist novel atmosphere he'd had in mind since morning, with that indispensable comic touch found in all literary masterpieces.

Toward nighttime, just before six, he returned home dazed from cigarettes and beer, and a little bloated. A little depressed, too. He had no desire to work on the novel because he couldn't remember a thing. He decided to eat dinner and go to bed.

When this Vincenzo Cusiani passed away, his papers were discovered; his family and everyone from the cafe had considered him a writer, but were under the impression that he refused to publish on principle. In his bureau there was a stack of writings. It was the famous novel *Ernesto*, which consisted of a page that started from the beginning over and over. It started at around nine in the morning and continued at the cafe and then it would trail off. Sometimes almost near the bottom of the page appeared the bartender who served the beer;

in real life, the bartender's name was Giuseppe, but in the novel he had the fictional name Pietro. *Pietro pours Ernesto a beer. Ernesto drinks it.* Or . . . *Ernesto raises the glass to his lips*. There wasn't a single sheet that went beyond that. The formal variations, as you can see, were minimal.

THE USE OF MAGNETS TO TREAT MORBID FIXATIONS

Dr. Maggiani, pharmacist, was the great-grandnephew of a Maggiani, phreniatrist, who around 1890 studied the effect of magnets on the nervous system, both of men and animals, and in one of his papers recommended them to combat morbid fixations. The manuscript of this paper has been preserved by the family and is still in their possession.

The great-grandnephew, the pharmacist, had a wife who after her first childbirth constantly heard creaking all around her and concluded that the end of the world was nigh. This was a morbid fixation, and thus kept her in an anxious state of agitation. She performed the household chores in great haste saying there was so little time already, as the walls and chairs were creaking terribly, and cracks were forming between the floor tiles. Then she would dash into the kitchen, and if for example it was lunchtime, she breaded and fried the veal in such a rush it was as if the kitchen wasn't going to be there much longer; and to cook even faster she'd heat the oil at such a high temperature it splattered everywhere and burned her hands. But her morbid fixation would complete its cycle, and suddenly everything seemed pointless and vain, so imminent was the world's end. And the veal seemed pointless to her too, so she sat down and let it burn.

Her husband, Dr. Maggiani, would say, "Why do you always think the world is going to end at lunch?" He said this because he was sick of burnt veal. Even the spaghetti was always far overcooked, as his wife, after flinging it into the bubbling water like a madwoman and urging it to boil, was beset by the morbid fixation that the world was going to end much sooner than eight minutes, the recommended cooking time for the spaghetti; so she kept watching it boil without doing anything else, waiting for the stove along with the entire kitchen to collapse. At that point someone else in the house would come and turn off the stove. "Please," her husband said, "if you're not up for it, you don't have to cook." Indeed, there was the mother-in-law living with them. The mother-in-law's opinion was that her daughter-in-law didn't really know her way around a kitchen. And it was for precisely this reason, to prove the contrary at least one last time, that upon hearing the clock tower strike twelve the daughter-in-law rushed to the kitchen and turned on the stove. She could have made some decent dishes, but they ended up dry or burnt, with her forlornly sitting on a chair, passively watching them burn. It was always the mother-in-law who saved a chicken from the oven or some meatballs from the flames. Dr. Maggiani hoped to disabuse her of this idea with logical reasoning, not yet having understood that it was actually a morbid fixation. "The world," he told her, "will surely come to an end, but it won't be sudden, because first the graves have to come open and the dead rise one by one. So there's plenty of time to cook, eat, and take a little afternoon nap." But a morbid fixation won't listen to reason, and in fact Mrs. Maggiani considered her husband an irresponsible, ordinary fool. The mother-in-law didn't interject so that no one could say mother- and daughter-in-law didn't get along, but she was of the opinion that there was no end of days without the dead rising first. In other words, she believed that her daughter-in-law's view was wrong.

That, therefore, was the situation, and there was no solution in sight, at least not until Mr. Maggiani turned to the magnet (or lodestone) after the great-uncle's theories. The theories were a little anachronistic, but contained all the indications of the specific type of morbid fixation described by the great-uncle. So Maggiani took his wife to the back of the pharmacy, where there was an exam table. "Lie down!" he told her. The wife lay down. The manuscript said that subjects were to lie down. "Close your eyes." The instruction was that patients needed to be in a docile mental state. The wife closed her eyes but said, "Hurry up, hurry up"—she could feel the world coming apart. Then, Dr. Maggiani applied the magnet; it was wrapped in white gauze to hide it from view. He applied it to her head, at the occiput. The magnet weighed four hundred grams and came from an auto shop. Magnets aren't readily sold as objects in themselves. There are small ones at stationery stores. But the first application has to be strong; therefore, it takes the kind of magnets found in the engine of a car or a truck.

After ten minutes, Dr. Maggiani asked, "What do you hear?" And his wife: "The world creaking." But she said it was no longer creaking so terribly; it actually seemed to be settling. "Seems like it's just squeaking," she said. The wife didn't know about the magnet. The patient can't know, because the morbid fixation could put up resistance to the magnetic field. She lay there for a few more minutes with the magnet applied, then she got up and said that she had been mistaken. For that, she was all happy. "The world goes on, it just squeaks a little," she explained to the husband. And the husband replied, "Naturally." "Like a wheelbarrow," the wife said. "Sure, like a wheelbarrow," replied the husband, in awe of the magnet's pull.

After that, whenever the wife was beset by the end of the world, he would lay her down and redirect her mind. It would happen suddenly and erratically, once every few days or months. And he gladly applied the magnet to his mother-in-law as well, when she started worrying about graves opening and the dead rising.

At certain moments Dr. Maggiani thought he'd hit on something big, scientifically speaking, heretofore undiscovered (except by his uncle). But as a pharmacist, he feared the medical establishment, and so he never came out with it. He only said that his uncle had had a connection with Freud, and he still had a letter from him dated 1918. His uncle was from Lavarone (where Freud would vacation) and spoke German; he had made some objections to the principles of psychoanalysis, and proposed alternatives, including magnets.

This reconstruction of events explains something that Maggiani in his advanced age was wont to say with conviction. He said, if magnets were more common, humanity would be better off.

SUPERNUMERARY EPILOGUE

On the outskirts of many cities, there are often elderly individuals of the male sex wandering around without identification in a state of general amnesia. Some are returned to relatives; others are never identified and nobody comes to claim them.

These are individuals who leave the house on impulse, and set off for a place but no longer remember where. They give the impression that they have some kind of appointment. Sometimes they walk a great distance. Some of them hop on the train without thinking. And they don't know which station they left from nor their destination. Usually they're found by the police and the exchange is always the same.

The unidentified individual, who appears to be about seventy, is taken down to headquarters. He's usually compliant. He is ushered into an office (as in the case being transcribed here). But the individual in question immediately looks for the exit. He walks right by without seeing it, then he goes into a corner of the room. He touches the corner and says: "This is a maze!"

He's led through the door. So he looks at it and says: "Finally! Is this the exit?"

When he's in the hallway, instead of walking down it he presses up against the wall, feeling around for something; then he says: "Where's the window?"

They tell him: "There are no windows." He looks perplexed. He adds: "But there used to be." Still leaning against the wall, groping around, he moves to the right. His knee hits a chair and immediately he starts kicking. With an alarmed expression, he says: "Whose cats are these? The doorman's?"

They tell him it's a chair. He laughs and says, "The doorman's chair."

They lead him down the hall. He resists a little and keeps saying, "Careful, careful! You want me to fall down the stairs?"

They tell him not to worry, there aren't any stairs. He seems reassured, but remains watchful. "These darned steps! If you're not careful you can miss them."

They accompany him to the missing persons office. They have him take a seat. He says: "It's so crowded! Are all these people waiting?" He greets someone to his right with a little wave, and says: "There's room, there's room right here," pointing to the wall.

They ask him his name. He says: "Boni, it's Boni." Then he gets up and says again: "It's so crowded! How can anybody stand it?"

They tell him he's the only one in there. He smiles at them with understanding and points to the right. "I've never seen so many people. Is there an audition?"

They tell him no. He seems satisfied.

"How old are you?" He thinks for a while. "My wife would know; I don't pay attention to such things." He is still gesturing for others to take a seat.

"Mr. Boni," they say, "what did you do in life?" He bows, touched. That word seems to have affected him. They repeat the question. He closes his eyes, almost crying. He says: "In life?" Tears slip out of his eyes. "What did I do? Very little. I swear."

"But what did you use to do?" they ask him. "Work in an office? Did you work in an office?" Right away he replies, "No, no, I swear."

"What did you do in life?" He looks around. He lowers his voice a little. "I didn't have time. It was so short." Then he repeats: "Life! Life is so short." He cries at the word life. He blows his nose. "You can even ask my wife," he adds. "She's more informed about these things." Then he looks to the right. "Where are they going?" He looks worried and says, turning right: "Where are you going?" He moves toward the corner of the room and touches the corner. "Where did the handle go?" he asks.

Generally, their identity and past are never discovered.

Jamie Richards is a translator and editor based in Milan, where she works for the Balzan Foundation. She has translated numerous modern Italian writers and cartoonists, and her work has appeared in periodicals such as *Words Without Borders*, *The Los Angeles Review of Books*, *The Massachusetts Review*, *Exchanges*, and *The Florentine Literary Review*. She holds an MFA in literary translation from the University of Iowa and a PHD in comparative literature from the University of Oregon.

WAKEFIELD GALLERIES

1 *Exemplary Departures*
Gabrielle Wittkop

2 *Odd Jobs*
Tony Duvert

3 *Imaginary Lives*
Marcel Schwob

4 *Psychology of the Rich Aunt: Being an Inquiry, in Twenty-Five Parts, into the Question of Immortality*
Erich Mühsam

5 *Brief Lives of Idiots*
Ermanno Cavazzoni